Out Of the Ashes

T.K. Chapin

Out of the Ashes

Copyright © 2015 T.K. Chapin

All rights reserved.

ISBN-13:
978-1517622442

ISBN-10:
1517622441

DEDICATION

Dedicated to my mother,

the woman who taught me

that all things are possible with God.

CONTENTS

DEDICATION iv

ACKNOWLEDGMENTS i

CHAPTER 1 2

CHAPTER 2 12

CHAPTER 3 20

CHAPTER 4 32

CHAPTER 5 50

CHAPTER 6 70

CHAPTER 7 83

CHAPTER 8 100

CHAPTER 9 113

CHAPTER 10 125

CHAPTER 11 130

CHAPTER 12 140

CHAPTER 13 151

CHAPTER 14 167

CHAPTER 15 179

CHAPTER 16	190
CHAPTER 17	205
CHAPTER 18	217
CHAPTER 19	232
CHAPTER 20	248
CHAPTER 21	257
Book Preview	268
Other Books	303
Author's Note	306
ABOUT THE AUTHOR	307

ACKNOWLEDGMENTS

First and foremost, I want to thank God. God's salvation through the death, burial and resurrection of Jesus Christ gives us all the ability to have a personal relationship with the creator of the Universe.

I also want to thank my wife. She's my muse and my inspiration. A wonderful wife, an amazing mother and the best person I have ever met. She's great and has always stood by me with every decision I have made along life's way.

I'd like to thank my editors and early readers for helping me along the way. I also want to thank all of my friends and extended family for the support. It's a true blessing to have every person I know in my life.

CHAPTER 1

Tapping on the bar top down at the Spark, I made eye contact with Lonzo and he knew exactly what I needed. Another Rum and Coke. I was bumping my head to the rhythm of the music as I waited for him to bring me my drink, when a woman approached me.

"My girlfriend told me that you're a firefighter... is that true?" she asked as her lip curled up on one side. She had that look in her eye, that same look I had seen a hundred times before. It's a mixture of drinking a little too much and infatuation.

"Your girlfriend is telling you the truth," I replied, grinning, as I turned around on the bar stool to face her. Suddenly Lonzo's hand came over my shoulder with a Rum and Coke.

"There you go, Kane," he said.

I grabbed the glass and took a sip. "Mmmm... perfect." Looking back at Lonzo, I nodded and said, "Thanks, Bro."

He nodded and continued down the bar to help other patrons of the Spark. Looking back at the woman, she suddenly didn't look so hot as she cupped her mouth and bent over.

"Bathrooms are that way," I said, pointing over to the corner.

She hurried her steps quickly away to the bathrooms, and I shook my head as I stood up and returned over to the pool table with Brian and the two girls we just had met earlier. The brunette who had been flirting with me all night, moseyed up to my side and grabbed onto my arm. Leaning into my ear, with a seductive voice, she said, "I hope that girl wasn't trying to steal my man away."

I laughed. "Sugar, I'm not your man." I glanced towards the bathrooms as I continued, "But

I wouldn't worry about her. I think the only date she'll have tonight is with a porcelain bowl."

Brian laughed as he came over and handed me a pool stick. "It's your shot, McCormick." I took a swig of my rum and coke and set it on the table next to me as I flashed a smile his way.

As I walked past Brian, I leaned into his ear and said, "Boys verses girls isn't very fair for them. Now is it?"

"True, but we are all trashed and nobody really cares," Brian replied, laughing as he lost his footing for a second.

I nodded in agreement as I strolled around the pool table. I decided to go for the six ball and got into position. I leaned across the worn green felt-top pool table and looked at the corner pocket. Glancing down at the cue ball, I lined up my shot and let it rip. As I stood upright, I felt my phone vibrate in my pocket. Pulling it out slightly, I saw it was my sister Emily. She rarely called and never at this time of night. Handing Brian my pool stick with a lowered brow, I said, "I'm going to step out for a moment. I'll be back."

"Alright, man. Everything cool?" Brian asked.

"Hope so," I replied. Turning, I headed out of the bar and out to the sidewalk as I answered my sister's call. "Ems?"

A sniffle came across the line setting my worry soaring and my pulse racing.

"What is it? What's wrong?" I asked.

"It's... mom."

I shook my head as I touched my forehead and looked down at the cracking pavement below my feet. "What do you mean, Emily? What's wrong with mom?"

She began crying for a moment before being able to squeeze out the words, "It's back."

The bar music and noises that were coming from a few feet away quieted as my world began to crumble at the words my sister spoke. My mother's cancer was back. "How bad?" I asked.

"Bad..." she replied, her words trailing off in her hopeless tone.

I sighed heavily as I looked up the sidewalk that was illuminated by the street lights. I wanted to start running right then and not stop until I reached my mother. "So, she'll need lots of chemo and more rounds of-"

"No!" Emily snapped, interrupting me.

"What?"

"It's not like that this time... It's bad, Kane... really bad. They aren't going to be treating the cancer."

I dipped my head and let my back fall against the brick wall that was behind me. "Really? They can't do anything? Surgery?"

"No... they already tried all they could. She kept it from us when it came back a few months ago. She didn't want to worry us. She has months to live... if she's lucky."

"I'm going to come over," I said sternly, wiping the falling tears from my eyes.

"No, don't do that... I'm okay, Kane."

"Well, I'm not. And judging by the phone call in the middle of the night and the crying, you aren't okay either. I want to be there for you, Sis."

She sniffled. "Thank you, but I'm okay. I know I made you feel bad for not being there for me after we found out about Kyle. But I'm older now and I understand. Plus, I'm at work right now."

"Kane!" Lonzo hollered from the doorway of the bar just a few paces from where I was standing.

Startled, I wiped my eyes quickly and stood

up straight. "What?"

"Your friend looks like he's in trouble," Lonzo replied.

Turning back to my conversation with Emily, I said, "I'll call you tomorrow."

"Take care of yourself, Kane," she replied.

I hung up with Emily and slipped the phone back into my pocket. As I approached the door, I looked at Lonzo. He looked worried. "What's going on?" I asked.

"I don't know. But the guy doesn't look too happy..."

"Where are they?" I asked, glancing in through the bar.

Lonzo pointed over to the pool tables as he rubbed the back of his neck. "Over there... I think it's one of those chicks' boyfriends."

I took a deep breath and gave him a nod. "I'll handle this." Walking past Lonzo, I made a beeline for the pool tables. I saw a big beefy bald guy cornering Brian. Pushing through the crowd of people, I grabbed onto his shoulder, yanked him around towards me, and said, "Hey! Back off!"

He turned around with a pool stick in his

meaty hand and laughed. Smacking the stick against the pool table, he broke it in half. As the broken pieces of the pool stick hit the floor, my heart began to race as adrenaline coursed through me. Holding the busted end of the stick up to my throat, he asked, "What are you going do about it?"

I shook my head and took a step back. "You don't want to mess with me right now," I warned.

He laughed again. "Oh yeah? You think you're a tough guy?"

I reached out and quickly grabbed the stick from his hands and flipped it around smacking him upside the head. He dropped to the ground with a loud thump. "Get out of here, Brian!" I shouted, pointing to the side door.

Brian grabbed his phone off the edge of the pool table and darted for the exit. As the door swung shut, the man I had smacked rose back to his feet. He paused to wipe a bit of the blood from his wound. Rubbing the blood between his thumb and index finger, the man looked up at me. His eyes were bloodshot red and eyebrows were furrowed. "Only one other man has ever made me bleed, he's dead now and you'll soon join him!"

Worry came over me as I thought about how ugly this could get, I didn't want anything to happen with my job. I decided to run. As I weaved between the crowd of people, I kept looking over my shoulder as the man pursued me. "Lonzo! Help!" I shouted as I looked over at the bar where I spotted him. Making it to the door, I fell out onto the sidewalk.

The man came outside and laughed as I squirmed to regain my footing. There was something wrong with my ankle and it wasn't allowing me to put any pressure on it to stand. "Look, dude, I was just trying to help my friend. You were cornering him!" I tried to plead with him.

"You don't put your lips on another man's girlfriend. He broke the rule," the man said as he came closer to me. He towered over me like a shadow of death.

Suddenly sirens came whipping around the corner and caused the guy to run. One of the three cop cars chased the man down the alley while the other two came up to the curb and parked.

I relaxed my head against the cold cement of the sidewalk and breathed a sigh of relief. My racing heart began to settle as the officers approached. Looking at them with an upside down view from the pavement, I noticed one of the cops that I had frequently seen on calls, Fred Foster. Worry came rushing in when I saw him. He hated me more than anyone else I knew in Spokane. Ever since his girlfriend kissed me at a joint Christmas party our stations had a few years back, the guy has been out to get me.

"That you, Kane?" Fred asked, approaching with a grin on his face. I began to attempt to get up. Fred and the officer with him helped me to my feet. Setting me down over at the curb, Fred laughed. "I always knew your lifestyle would catch up to you one day. You're screwed."

"C'mon now," I replied. "My buddy Brian was getting cornered by that guy who went running... there isn't anything illegal with what I did."

The other officer who was with Fred went inside the Spark as we continued speaking outside. "Well, that depends on what happened, Kane."

"Brian was backed into a corner and I interrupted the confrontation! I said that already."

"Regardless of the outcome. I have to report this to Chief Jensen."

I sighed and shook my head. "That's messed up."

"It's my duty to report it to your station Chief."

The other officer stepped out of the bar with the broken pool stick in hand. It had some of the blood from the man I had hit on it. Fred said, "Stand up. You're going in."

"C'mon! I was being threatened. He had it in his hand first."

"Doesn't matter. You're going in. You aren't even scratched." Fred turned me around as he undid his cuffs from his belt and began his spiel, "You have the right to remain silent..."

CHAPTER 2

The next morning I made my way down to the firehouse to start my shift. As I arrived in the kitchen to get some coffee, I found Cole making himself a bagel with cream cheese.

"Good morning, McCormick," he said as he lathered on the strawberry cream cheese.

"Morning," I replied, blinking my eyes rapidly to help push the sleep from them. Yawning, I poured myself a cup of coffee.

"You seem tired. Late night?" he asked.

I laughed a little as I brought the cup to my lips. Cole wasn't one to miss the little details. "You could say that..." I replied.

"What happened?" he asked as he put the cream cheese away in the fridge.

Shaking my head, I said, "Foster booked me."

Cole's eyes widened. "Seriously? For what?"

"Got into a bar fight at the Spark..."

"I thought you were putting that party lifestyle behind you, McCormick."

"Nah..." I replied. "That's the real reason why Ashley left me... I wasn't ready to give it up. But after this whole thing with my mom and going to jail, I don't know man... something's got to change."

"Wait, what's going on with your mom?"

I sniffed a little and turned to wipe away a quick tear that came on that I couldn't stop. Turning back to Cole, I said, "It's back..." I dipped my chin to my chest.

He came over and put a hand on my shoulder as he asked, "How bad is it?"

"It's terminal. She's got months," I replied,

shaking my head.

"I'm so sorry to hear that–" Cole started to say before being interrupted.

"McCormick," Chief Jensen said from the doorway. "My office, now."

"Okay," I replied.

He disappeared out of sight back down the hallway. Cole looked at me. "That's probably due to your arrest. What happened exactly?"

"Some beef-head was cornering Brian and I stepped in."

Cole nodded. "I'll be sure to talk to Jensen about it... but he's probably going to suspend you while he investigates."

Shaking my head, I said, "That's the last thing I need. I don't want to be suspended right now. I need work to keep my mind busy."

"I know, I'll do my best to make it as short as possible. Go see your mom, McCormick," Cole replied, patting my shoulder.

I left the kitchen and headed down the hallway to Jensen's office. Every step I took, fear clawed its way deeper into me. Knocking lightly on the door that was partially open, I stepped into

Jensen's office.

"Have a seat, McCormick," he said, motioning to the chair in front of his desk.

I took a seat and sat straight as a nail. "Yes, Sir."

"I guess you probably already know what this is about."

"The bar fight."

"Yeah. What happened? I have a report here that says you beat a man with a broken pool stick."

I scoffed. "That's because Foster has a vendetta against me! He's a crooked cop."

"Hey!" Jensen snapped. "I know you two got beef, but that doesn't mean you don't need to have respect for him."

"Okay. Sorry..." I adjusted in my seat. "So what happened was, Brian and I were at the Spark and I stepped out for a moment. When I got back inside Brian was cornered by some giant dude and I stepped in."

Jensen shook his head. "Brian can handle his own."

"He's like a little brother to me, Sir. He was

in trouble and he's one of us. I had to step in and intervene."

"Okay, what happened next?"

"The guy snapped a pool stick and held it up to my throat... I grabbed it and smacked him in the head."

Jensen nodded. "Why didn't you toss the pool stick? Why beat him?"

"Tossing it wouldn't have fixed the problem... at least not in my eyes."

"So you took matters into your own hands and hit the man in the head with a broken pool stick." Chief Jensen sighed heavily and leaned back in his chair as he tossed the report on his desk. "I have to suspend you while I get this sorted out, McCormick." His tone was sharp and I could feel his disappointment with every word.

I dipped my chin to my chest and said, "I'm sorry."

"Sorry doesn't clean up the mess you got yourself into. You know after that whole stupid thing at that one fire where you smashed that guy's TV? You were kept based on good behavior."

"Still? That was a long time ago..."

"Doesn't matter. It's on your record."

"Okay... Well, I'm sorry."

"Stop apologizing and go home. I'll give you a call once I figure out what I can do." The Chief turned in his chair to indicate he was done with the discussion.

"Alright," I replied, standing up.

I left out of his office and back down the hallway. Going into the kitchen, I poured out the cup of coffee I had poured earlier. Cole came in from the dining hall and Brian from the hallway.

"How did it go?" Cole asked.

I set the cup in the sink and turned to him. "You were right, I'm suspended... I'm going to head up to Colville and see my mom."

"Dude... that sucks so bad you got suspended," Brian said.

"Yeah," I replied. Looking at Brian, I said, "Thanks for bailing me out of jail last night, I don't think I mentioned it in the cab."

Brian shook his head. "Don't worry about it. What'd you do to that cop to get him so angry?"

Cole laughed as he poured a refill of his

coffee and headed out of the dining room.

"His girlfriend kissed me at a joint Christmas party our stations were having. I didn't initiate, but he caught the tail end of it and was pretty upset."

"That's no reason to illegally detain you," Brian replied.

I shrugged. "I don't think it's technically illegal what he did. I did bust the pool stick over the dude's head and didn't have a scratch on me."

"Yeah. Is Captain Taylor going to put in a good word for you with the Chief?"

"Of course. He knows me... So does the Chief, though. So I don't know how it'll turn out. Chief mentioned an old incident still being on my record..."

"Lame," Brian replied.

Cole peeked back into the kitchen and said, "McCormick, let your mom know I'm praying for her. And let me know if you need anything at all. You're doing the right thing going up there."

"Thanks," I replied. Watching as Cole returned to the dining hall, I saw Micah join him at the table. Turning to Brian, I said, "Let the other guys know what's going on, would you?"

He nodded. "Will do. Take care." He patted me on the shoulder as he went into the dining hall.

"Thank you." I headed out of the kitchen and down the steps of the firehouse to head to Colville and see my mother. It wasn't a trip I was looking forward to taking, but I knew I had to make the journey to see her.

CHAPTER 3

Pulling into the gravel driveway at my mom's had never been more terrifying. I have visited her when she had cancer, but never with the mindset of her not being around in a few months. I felt like a scared little boy about to lose his mom and I didn't know how to deal with the emotions that came with it. Part of me wanted to scream and freak out and the other part of me didn't even want to be there.

  Roofus, the golden retriever that my mother has had forever, came running from the doorway of my mom's house as she pushed open the screen door. I smiled as Roofus ran up to me as I got out of my car. Bending a knee, I rubbed behind both of Roofus' ears.

Walking up the rest of the driveway, I crossed over the lawn and to the front steps.

"Hello, Kane," my mother said from the doorway in a delicate tone as she coughed and covered her mouth.

"Mother," I replied as I took my steps up the porch to her. Giving her a hug triggered my mind to race. I wondered how many hugs were left before she'd be gone forever. Breaking away from our embrace, she led me inside and sat down on the same old couch that she'd had since the seventies.

"How are you feeling?" I asked as I crossed my legs over, getting comfortable.

She shrugged and smiled. "I'm fine. Do you want some coffee or chocolate milk?"

I smiled. "Coffee's good, Mom. Thanks."

"I put on a pot when you called and said you were coming up to see me."

I nodded as I watched her get up and head into the kitchen. She reached into the cupboard and began to pull down a cup. "Your sister Emily won't stop calling me. I'm pretty sure she calls between seeing every patient of hers. She knew I was up last night and she wouldn't stop calling."

"That's right, she was working last night," I replied.

She nodded as she brought my cup of coffee back over to me. "Her working last night was the only reason why she even found out about my cancer. She ran into one of her friends who saw me in the oncology wing of the hospital when I was down there last week."

"Ahhh..." I replied as I took a sip of my coffee. My mother wasn't much of a coffee drinker and she didn't really understand that one little scoop wasn't enough coffee to make a strong pot. My cup was practically see-through from how weak it was, but I didn't mention it.

"That Christopher. I sure do worry about him ever since Emily and Andy broke up."

"He's thirteen years old, Mother," I replied. "I think he's old enough to understand what's going on."

"Yeah! That's exactly the problem! He's fully aware... I remember when your father left us, your sister was that same age. She got into quite a bit of trouble in those years."

Intrigued that my perfect sister did anything wrong, I asked, "Really?" I set my coffee down on the end table and leaned in closer to my mother to hear more.

"Yep. I don't ever talk about it... because there is no reason to do so, but she went through quite the rebellious phase. Drugs, drinking and boys... It was bad."

"How did I not know about this?" I asked, setting my cup down on the coffee table.

"Well, you were only seven-years-old, Kane. And I did my best to keep it away from you."

I nodded. "Makes sense. How did she grow out of that stage?"

"Well, I was running out of options on what to do and finally tried church. She got into the youth group there and loved it. She gave up on all the bad friends and gravitated to the new ones."

"Strange, since she loathes God," I replied.

My mother nodded and then shook her head. "It's too bad... but that change away from God was all from that stupid boy, Andy." My mother shook her head again. "I hate that man... and you know I don't like using that word!"

I nodded, but didn't have a response.

"Anyways..." she said, letting her face soften back into a smile. "I'm so happy you came to visit your old mom."

"Of course. I love you, Mom... and I'm worried about you. How are you handling everything?"

"I'm okay," she replied, placing a hand on my knee. "I know where I'm going." She glanced up at the ceiling. "I'm going to meet Jesus and see your brother again," she declared, raising her hands up and shaking them in the air. "Hallelujah!" she shouted.

My eyebrows shot up and I laughed. "Put your hands down, Mom!"

She laughed, "How come?"

"I don't know... but it's weird." I picked up my coffee and took a drink.

Her eyes followed my movements as I set the cup back down on the coffee table. She said, "Son, you've got some talking to do with your Creator."

I smiled. "Maybe. But I'm here with you right now. So, I'll stick with talking to you."

"Okay," she replied, letting the topic of God slip away. "Back to Christopher. I think you should take him for a few days when you can... he'd do good to have a solid man in his life."

I nodded. "I wouldn't mind doing that... I'm sure Emily wants to come spend some time alone with you, anyway. It would all work out pretty nicely."

My mother smiled and nodded. "Yeah, that'd be nice."

No matter how much I enjoyed it, sitting there talking with my mother was bittersweet. The thought of not knowing how much longer I could do this with her was always in the back of my mind.

On my way back to Spokane, I honored my mother's wishes and called Emily and pitched her the idea of taking Christopher for a few days. She agreed without hesitation.

Upon arriving at Emily's, I saw a Honda in the driveway I didn't recognize. It was white and an older model similar to the old one I had back in High School. Parking alongside the curb, I got out of my car and took off my shades.

I walked up to the front door and gave it a

firm knock. Hearing footsteps just beyond the door, my curiosity was piqued. Leaping off the cement porch and into the flower bed, I peeked in the living room window to see what was going on. Spotting Christopher and some other kid shoving stuff under a couch, I knocked on the window and got their attention.

Pointing over to the door to indicate I wanted Christopher to answer it, he nodded and headed that way. He opened up the door and said, "Hey, Uncle Kane... what are you doing here?"

I could smell pot lingering just on the other side of him. "Your mom didn't tell you I was coming to pick you up?"

He shook his head and said, "No."

"Oh... well... that's what is happening."

He sighed and looked over his shoulder at his friend. "Yo, Kegan. You gotta bounce. I'm going to my uncle's house."

The kid nodded and grabbed his backpack from the floor and headed out the door to his Honda in the driveway. As Kegan opened his driver side door, he spotted my car –a yellow with black racing stripes, 1979 Shelby Mustang— at the curb. He looked back at me and said, "Sick ride!"

I nodded to him and said, "We'll see you later, Kegan."

He nodded and got into his car and left.

"Why you gotta be rude to my friend?" Christopher asked.

"I can smell the pot, moron. Grab your stuff and let's go." I turned and went back out to my car. On the way down the sidewalk out to the curb, I couldn't help but feel bad for my sister. I should have been around more for her over the years. Knowing his father, Andy, wasn't involved much, I could have done something.

While I waited for Christopher to come out, I saw an elderly man walking down the sidewalk across the street. He had a backpack and an old wooden stick as a cane. What intrigued me most was the ridiculous smile he kept on his face and he would wave to every car that passed by him.

As Christopher climbed into my car, I pointed to the man walking. "Who is that?"

Christopher laughed. "That's Old Man Smiles. He walks up and down this street, and around the neighboring roads just smiling and waving to all the cars that pass by."

"Interesting. Why?" I asked.

"Nobody knows," Christopher replied fastening his seat belt.

"Strange," I replied, turning the key over. "You shouldn't do drugs Christopher... they kill those brain cells and ruin your life."

"It was my friend. I wasn't doing it... I swear," he replied, raising his hands in defense.

I glared over at him as I searched his eyes. There weren't any indicators I could spot, so I dropped it. "Okay, I hope not."

"Man, I love this car," Christopher said as the engine hummed. "What kind of car is it?" he asked.

"A '79 Shelby Mustang. They don't make them like this anymore," I replied, grinning as I dropped my shades over my eyes and put the car into drive.

We made a stop at the grocery store on the way home to pick up a few essentials. Soda, treats and frozen pizzas were among the plans to keep Christopher's ravenous teenager appetite at bay.

As we were walking down one of the aisles in the store, I spotted a pretty blonde attempting to reach for something on a top shelf. I wasn't going to intervene, but then she stood on the bottom shelf to help herself reach for the item she was after.

"Hello, Ma'am?" I said, approaching her.

She looked over her shoulder at me. "What?" she asked, sounding annoyed I was even speaking with her.

Sensing the distrust in her tone, I tried to reason with her the best I could. "That doesn't look very safe. Can I help you?"

She jumped backwards off the bottom shelf and landed on her feet. "Sure," she replied with a shrug. "It's the bow-tie noodles in the back..."

I pushed myself up onto my toes and leaned back to grab the box. As I came back down, she said, "Thank you..."

"You're welcome," I replied. Christopher and I continued down the aisle until we made our way around the corner when Christopher looked over at me with a questioning expression.

"Why didn't you get her number?" he asked.

Startled by his question, I stopped the cart and looked at him. "Why would you ask that?"

"Well, mom says all you do is drink beer and pick up chicks."

"She told you that?" I asked, surprised.

"Well, no. Not exactly. I heard her on the phone with one of her friends."

"Of course you did..." I replied as I started pushing the cart again. I loved my sister, but surgeon or not when it came to common sense, she was dumb as a box of rocks. Christopher wasn't a baby anymore. He could hear things, and even I, without children, knew that.

As I put away the groceries back at my apartment, Christopher sat on a barstool up at the island in the kitchen.

"Hey, Uncle Kane?" he asked.

"Yeah?" I replied, as I put away the pizzas into the freezer.

"What's going to happen to Grandma?" he asked.

I stopped as I shut the freezer door and

turned around to him. Walking over to the island, I leaned across the countertop and said, "What makes you ask that?"

He opened up the sticky bun he had on the counter in front of him and said, "I heard mom on the phone this morning when she came by the house to shower. Is Grandma going to be okay?"

"Grandma's not doing so hot, kid," I replied, letting my finger trace circles on top of the counter. Looking up at him, I saw the worry run across his face. Glancing over at the TV just beyond the couch behind Christopher, I said, "Let's play some games and relax for the rest of the evening. How's that sound?"

He smiled and nodded. "Do you have the newest Holodeck?"

I nodded. "Of course. Go ahead and go import your profile, I'll toss a pizza in the oven for dinner." He jumped up and went into the living room. That evening we played video games until one o'clock in the morning, not speaking another word on the matter of my mother's health.

CHAPTER 4

As I rolled out of bed the next day, I could see partially down the hallway and into the living room. Christopher was already awake and playing more video games.

I yawned as I came out into the living room and strolled into the kitchen. "Bit early for games, don't you think?" I asked.

He shrugged and said over his shoulder, "I'm an early riser. Nothing else to do."

I tilted my head back and forth, mulling his response over in my mind. "Makes sense," I replied. In the kitchen, I grabbed for the coffee can from the cupboard and pulled it down. As I was scooping the coffee grounds into the pot, the power suddenly cut out.

"What happened?" Christopher asked from the couch.

"Looks like the power went out," I replied. Walking over to my sliding glass door off the kitchen, I glanced outside across the balcony to the neighboring apartments. Spotting Mr. Berry's TV off –which was never off— and Mr. Berry screaming into his phone, I said, "Looks like everyone lost their power in the complex."

"When will it be back on? I was in the middle of a mission..." Christopher replied, annoyed.

"No need to panic, Christopher. It'll come back on when it comes back on. Really depends on why it happened." I returned to the kitchen and continued scooping coffee into the basket of the coffee pot. Filling it with water, Christopher got off the couch and came into the kitchen.

"Why are you making coffee? You can't brew it."

"Well, I'm hopeful this will be resolved soon

and I can just turn on the coffee pot." I smiled at him as I pushed the coffee pot back up against the back splash.

Christopher sighed. "This sucks," he said, heading back over to the couch, and plopping down dramatically.

"Yeah, I'll call the electric company and see what's going on."

"Alright," he replied with another heavy sigh. He pulled out his cell phone and began playing a game, while I found the number on a bill from the counter for the electric company.

I called and immediately was greeted by a front end message. "Our records indicate there is a large scale power outage in the area in which you are calling from. The estimated time of fix is unknown. If this is the reason you are calling, please hang up now otherwise press 2."

I hung up. "Looks like it'll be out for a bit... it's a large scale outage and there is no ETA."

"Really?" Christopher said, keeping his eyes glued to his cell phone's screen.

"Yep," I replied with a sigh.

His phone suddenly shut off. "Great. And I forgot to charge my phone last night... Lame." He sighed yet again, tossing his phone to the other end of the couch. I walked into the living room and sat down beside him. "That's alright, we'll figure something out."

"What's wrong with Grandma exactly?" he asked. "Other than the fact she's not doing so hot or whatever that stupid response was you gave me yesterday..."

"Hey now. Stop with the 'stupid' and 'sucks' comments. But to answer your question..." I paused for a moment as I tried to figure out how to continue. "I don't know if you're old enough to know this kind of thing, or what your mom would want... but I'm going to tell you anyways. Your Grandma McCormick is dying from cancer. She doesn't have much time to live..."

"What?" he asked, his eyes welled with tears. "She's going to die? Aren't there doctors and medicine to fix this kind of thing?" he asked.

I shook my head. "The cancer has spread too much for them to help. They've already tried everything that they can do."

He sat back into the couch and dipped his chin. Softly, he said, "So just like that she's going to die..."

"Yeah..." I replied, feeling uncomfortable

with his sadness. Thinking about my mother and how she mentioned Heaven, I used her own words and said, "She's going to go to Heaven and be with Uncle Kyle."

He shook his head and stood up from the couch. "Mom says there is no such thing as Heaven." He left the living room and went into my bedroom, slamming the door behind him. I cringed at the sound. I went down the hallway and to the door. Leaning an ear against the grain, I listened. Hearing him sobbing softly to himself, I recalled my childhood and how I took everything my mother said at face value. I suspected that's what Christopher was doing, too. Knowing his father was absent from his life and his mother was busy with work all the time, I felt it was my duty in that moment to step up and be there for him.

I knocked on the door lightly and turned the doorknob as I walked in. "Christopher..." I said as I came to the edge of the bed where he was sitting.

"What?" he asked, turning away from me slightly.

I placed a hand on his shoulder and said, "Heaven's real and Grandma and Kyle are going to be there waiting for the rest of us."

He looked up at me and shook his head. "I don't know if I believe that." He turned away from me and fixed his sights on the wall.

Glancing over in the direction of Christopher's gaze, I saw my glove and baseball bat lying on the floor. He's just a kid, I thought to myself. He shouldn't be wallowing in sorrow. "You ever played baseball?" I asked.

"No," he replied. Something must have intrigued him about the sport, because he turned to me and asked, "You play?"

"Sometimes... All the guys at the fire station and I went and played a few weeks back."

He wiped his eyes and stood up from the bed. Going over to the glove, he picked it up and turned to me. "Well, we can't do anything here at the apartment. Can we go play?"

I nodded, thinking about all that activity without an ounce of coffee in me. "I haven't had my morning java... but I guess I can grab some on the way."

"Awesome! Can I use this mitt?" he asked, looking at it.

"Sure... or we could get you your own at the store?"

He smiled. "I'd like that."

"Let's go down to the garage and see if we can find the bucket of balls I couldn't find the other day."

"Alright," Christopher replied.

We left the apartment and put the baseball bat and glove in the car before heading over to the garage. Unlocking the garage door, we both lifted up on each side and pushed it open. An earthy smell filled our noses as we walked into the garage.

"It smells like dirt in here," Christopher said, covering his nose.

"Yeah, I noticed that the other day when I was in here after that big thunderstorm. There's a leak up in the roof and every time it rains, it gets that earthy-smell."

"You should fix it," Christopher replied, picking up a bale hook off of a shelf.

"Yeah. I plan on it..." I said, walking over to him. "You know what that is?" I asked as he inspected it.

"Looks like something out of a horror movie, honestly," he replied, handing it to me.

I laughed. "Yeah. It looks like that, but it's actually a bale hook. It was from a summer when I was about your age. I was visiting my Uncle Roy out in Chattaroy after my mother was too overwhelmed with one of her latest boyfriend's ditching out on her."

"Really?" Christopher asked as he continued looking around the garage. "I could never picture you doing anything on a farm..."

"It was a long time ago..." I smiled as I reflected back on the first time I had ever used it. It was on a trip with Roy to pick up some hay from a farm out in the middle of nowhere in Idaho.

Breaking into my thoughts, Christopher said, "Found the bucket of balls."

Glancing over at him as he was crouched under the workbench, I saw he had moved a stack of newspapers out of the way. "Ah... I'm bad at looking behind things."

"That's probably why you missed it the other day," Christopher replied as I set the bale hook back down on the shelf.

"Yeah, probably," I replied with a grin. "Let's get going," I said, walking out of the garage. Christopher grabbed the bucket of balls and I shut the door. As I was locking it, Christopher turned to look at me.

"Do you go to church?" he asked.

I looked over at him, surprised. "What happened to the days when you just wanted some candy and a hug?" I asked, smiling.

"I grew up. I'm an adult now."

"Don't try so hard to be an adult. It's not all it's cracked up to be." I finished locking the garage door and turned around to head for my car. "As far as church goes... I haven't been in a while..."

"Since you and Ashley broke up?" Christopher asked as we walked.

I stopped and looked at him. "You know about us breaking up? You hear that from your mom too?"

He laughed, shaking his head. "I saw your relationship status update online."

Smiling I replied, "Oh, yeah. I forgot I did that. But anyway, yes, haven't been going since then."

By the time we arrived at the park, the early morning coolness burned off and the sun was beating down on the back of our necks.

"It's hot out here," Christopher said as we strolled up to the baseball field.

"Yeah, roll up your jeans. It'll keep you cooler," I suggested.

"That's stupid, I'll look like an idiot," Christopher replied.

I shrugged. "Suit yourself. Be hot and sweaty while you look *cool*."

"I will," he replied. "Can I throw first?"

I was surprised by his desire to throw instead of hit. I recalled being a teenager and always wanting to bat, never throw. "Yeah, sure... why don't you want to bat?"

"I want to try this mitt out," Christopher replied, looking down at his glove on his hand. Smiling, he said, "It feels so cool on my hand... like a glove!"

"That's the idea behind the baseball *glove*," I replied, grinning. "You need some help throwing?" I asked.

"No. I'm okay. I have thrown stuff around before. I'm not that much of a noob. Just haven't played baseball..." Christopher split off from me as we walked the field, and jogged over to the pitcher's mound with the bucket of balls.

"Okay," I replied, taking to the plate with my bat in hand. Getting into position, I lifted the bat up onto my shoulder and said, "Toss it."

He threw the ball so hard that it would have given me a concussion if it would have hit me in the head. Luckily, I ducked out of the way and dropped to the dirt before it had a chance to land.

"Sorry," he said, turning beet red in embarrassment.

"Jeez!" I shouted, with a smile so I didn't discourage him. "A little softer and straighter over the plate..."

"I guess I don't know my own strength," Christopher laughed.

"Yeah, that's it..." I replied, smiling as I stood up and picked up my shades off the dirt beside the plate. "Maybe try under hand."

"Alright." He lobbed another one, this one went off course, but I was able to run across the plate and hit the ball, sending a grounder to him. He ran over and scooped it up into his glove.

"Got it!" he said, overly excited.

"Good job," I replied, walking back over to the plate.

"I want to try batting now."

"Alright. Want help with that?" I asked as I walked out to the pitcher's mound.

He shook his head. "I want to at least try on my own first."

"Okay," I replied as I handed him the bat and took his glove. I set his glove down next to the bucket of baseballs and grabbed my mitt from the other side of the bucket. Sliding my fingers into the glove, I grabbed a ball and got into position to throw.

"Ready," he said, from the plate. His form wasn't horrible, I thought to myself.

I tossed the ball underhand to him and he swung too early, missing the ball. I jogged up to him and stood out in front of him. I said, "Right when you see the ball in this area, you swing... You gotta swing before the ball gets to you, but not too early.... Make sense?"

"Yeah," he replied as I started back.

"And..." I said, turning and jogging back up to him. "Swing like this." I took the bat and showed him how to follow through on the swing.

"Okay," he said, nodding.

I ran back to the mound and grabbed another ball from the bucket. "Get ready."

He adjusted his footing and looked at me. He gave me a confirming nod.

I lobbed the ball underhand, nice and slow just like before and he smacked it. The ball went soaring into the outfield. Seeing a kid about Christopher's age just over the fence, I looked back and said, "I'll get it. I'm going to see if that kid wants to play." Setting my mitt down on the bucket of balls, I jogged out to the outfield where the ball and the kid were.

"Hey," I said, as I approached and put my shades on my head. "You want to play with us?" I picked up the baseball.

He shrugged and looked over his shoulder for a moment before looking back at me. "Sure..."

"You don't have to play if you don't want to," I said.

"No, I want to play. I just don't have a mitt here right now..."

"Well, you can use one of ours," I said.

"Okay, cool..." he replied, smiling as he came

over to me.

"There's a mitt over by the bucket you can use."

"Thanks. And I just want to catch out in the outfield, no batting."

I nodded. "Okay. That's fine by me."

"Cool, thanks."

"I'm Kane and that's Christopher over at the plate," I said.

"I'm Blake," the kid replied as he rushed past me through the grass over to grab the glove by the pitcher's mound. As I walked back to the mound, I saw Blake walk over and exchange hello's with Christopher.

We played through the early afternoon until about one o'clock. Taking a breather, I saw a woman come strolling up the park's path to the baseball field.

Blake left the glove behind in the outfield, dashing over to her. As I walked over to greet her, I realized it was the same woman from the store yesterday and I couldn't help myself from smiling. "Bow-tie pasta lady," I said as I took off my shades and glove and waved.

"Hi, again," she replied, smiling.

"I hope it was okay we were playing with Blake. He's really good at catching pop fly's," I said.

"He played outfield last year for his school. He loves it."

"I see..." I replied. "Is the power back on yet?" I asked.

She nodded. "That was bizarre, wasn't it?"

"Yeah, super strange. That outage is how we ended up out here playing baseball." I extended a hand out to shake hers. "I'm Kane by the way."

She smiled and shook my hand, "I'm Kristen."

"Nice to meet you. We were thinking about getting a bite to eat, Did you guys want to join us?" I asked, looking at her and then over at Blake. For some reason, unbeknownst to me, I really thought she would say yes.

"We were just about to go eat with some friends from church, but thank you for the offer," Kristen replied.

"Where do you go to church?" I asked, trying not to pry but not ready to say goodbye yet.

"Valley Baptist," she replied.

"I went there a few times and then switched over to Christ Community just up the road."

"That's Pastor Rick over there, right?" she asked.

I nodded. "Yep."

"You don't go to church, though," Christopher chimed in.

I went red in embarrassment. "I just haven't been in a while," I replied to Christopher.

"You and your son should come to the youth group barbeque tomorrow we are having at the church," she said.

I shook my head, "This isn't my son; he's my nephew."

"Oh, okay. You and your nephew should come," Kristen said.

"What time is that at? What's it involve exactly?" I asked.

"It's at four. There will be a barbeque, football and lots of God's people just hanging out and fellowshipping."

"Football?" I asked, with a raised brow. "That

sounds like it could be fun."

She smiled. "I think it's for the youth only..."

"Oh... yeah... right." I looked over at Christopher for his opinion on the matter. He nodded over at me with a smile. Looking back at Kristen, I said, "Sounds good... we'll be there."

"Great," she replied. Her phone began ringing and she pulled it out of her pocket. "That's our friends we are meeting for lunch. It was nice meeting you," she said, putting her hand over Blake's shoulder to usher him away.

"Nice meeting you too," I said, shooting her a quick wave as I watched her walk down the sidewalk. Turning my attention back to Christopher, I said, "Power is back on. Want to go back home and get some gaming in?"

He shook his head. "I'm having fun out here. Let's go get some food and come back and play some more?"

I nodded as a grin broke out on my face. "Sounds good, bud."

We walked to the parking lot and loaded our equipment into the back seat. Glancing over at Christopher in the passenger seat as I started the car, I thought again about him just being a kid. I said, "If you ever need someone to hang out with or talk to, you can call me."

"Okay," he said with zero emotion. I glanced over once more to catch a smile from the corner of his lip. I knew right at that moment, that I had made a connection with him. After lunch, we came back to the baseball field and played until nightfall. It was one of the most memorable times I ever had with Christopher.

There were no cell phones, electricity or other outside distraction. It was nothing like what Christopher and I were accustomed to in a world full of distractions. With only God's warmth from the sun, the dirt beneath our shoes, and each other, it was an unforgettable treasure in the sands of time.

CHAPTER 5

Smells of summertime filled the air as I got out of my car the next day at Valley Baptist. Looking over the top of my car over at Christopher, I saw him smile as he took a deep breath in through his nostrils inhaling the whiff of barbecuing in the distance.

"Smells good, doesn't it?" I asked.

He nodded. "I'm sick of frozen pizzas..." he paused for a moment. "No offense."

I shook my head as I shut the car door. "None taken. I don't care for my cooking abilities, or lack thereof. Nobody down at the fire station does either..." I laughed as I came around to the front of the car.

"Are my eyes deceiving me?" a man from across the parking lot asked as he hurried his steps across the pavement.

Christopher and I stopped and looked over at him. "Excuse me?" I asked, confused.

"Is that a '79 Shelby?" the man asked as he arrived over to us.

Glancing over my shoulder at my car, I nodded. Looking back at the stranger, I smiled and pushed up my shades to sit on top of my head. "Sure is... You into cars?" I asked.

Nodding, he replied, "I have a '69 Charger I've been working on forever. Just sits in my garage collecting dust for the most part, unfortunately." Walking up and alongside my car, he continued, "This car is the exact model my father had when I was growing up..."

"It's a nice car."

He seemed to be taken back for a moment with his thoughts and then suddenly he shook it off and extended a hand to me. "I'm so sorry. I didn't even introduce myself. I'm Tyson, Tyson Werstley," he said.

I shook his hand, "Kane McCormick, and this here is my nephew Christopher."

He shook Christopher's hand and said, "I have a boy about your age. He's with some of the youth group setting up for a LAN party this evening. You into video games?"

Christopher nodded. "Yeah, video games are cool. I've been to a couple of LAN parties, that's awesome that they are doing one."

"Yeah," Tyson replied, glancing at his watch. "They should be here soon. Are you guys new here?" Tyson asked as we began walking towards the side of the church.

I shook my head. "We don't attend here, just got an invite from Kristen."

"Oh, you know Kristen?" he asked, surprise evident on his face.

"Yeah, kinda... We were playing baseball with her son Blake," I replied.

Tyson nodded as he said, "Blake and my boy Tyler play together all the time. They're together right now at the LAN thing."

"Oh," I replied.

We came around to the backside of the church and found a rather large crowd of people. Rows of picnic tables were full of attendees. Several barbeques were off to one side. As Tyson split off from us and vanished into the sea of people, we walked by the grills. One man cooking looked over his shoulder and smiled as he nodded to us.

"These people seem pretty nice," I said.

He replied, "Yeah. Everyone is smiling... What are they so happy about."

I shrugged. "Kind of always like this at churches."

The smells were intoxicating and reminded me of how much I missed Gus' cooking at the firehouse. He had left the fire station a few months back after getting a cooking gig in Seattle for a fancy restaurant.

Christopher leaned over into my ear as we were about to a large pine tree, and asked, "When do you think we'll eat?"

I pulled my phone out of my pocket and checked the time. "Can't be long now... it's already a little after four o'clock."

He nodded and sighed. Arriving to the tree

that towered over the building as it leaned slightly to one side, we sat down at the base. I looked across the crowd as they all were deep in conversation and laughter. The atmosphere that these people created was warm and inviting. One lady appeared to be going from table to table organizing the salads and chips. Spotting Christopher and myself, she darted over to us.

"Welcome," she said with a genuine smile on her face. "I'm Leanne Barnes. I saw you two sitting over here. Are you new?"

"We were invited by Kristen," I replied.

"Oh, okay. She's a nice gal. What are your names?" Leanne asked.

"I'm Kane, and this here is Christopher."

"Well, It's nice to meet the both of you and I'm happy you came. We're fixing to eat here in a few minutes, so hopefully you two brought your appetites!"

"We sure did!" Christopher said, smiling.

"Good," she replied.

Someone called to her from one of the picnic tables in the crowd. "I better get going, but I hope to see you around at church sometime!" she said as she jogged back to her post at the tables.

I nodded to her and watched as she hurried her footsteps into the crowd. Christopher asked, "You think she gets paid well to help out?"

I shook my head. "Nobody really gets paid at most churches outside of the pastor."

Christopher's eyes widened. "Seriously? Why on earth do they do it?"

"They want to serve God, Christopher."

He didn't have a response and just nodded as he looked out into the football field that sat over in the distance.

"Hey, what's a LAN party?" I asked.

He laughed, looking back over at me. "Are you serious?"

I nodded, embarrassed by his shocked response. "Never heard of it before."

He adjusted in his seat to explain. "Basically, it's a bunch of gaming systems hooked up together so you can play with each other. It's really fun. I've been to a few of them."

"Why don't you go tonight with Blake and the others?" I asked.

He shook his head. "Not really something

you invite yourself to."

"How come?"

He shrugged. "Just not how it works."

"From the sounds of it, it'd be more fun the more people you have at one. Right?"

"It is more fun with more people, but that doesn't mean you want someone there that just invited himself. It'd be awkward."

"McCormick!" a man's familiar voice from the crowd shouted.

I shot a quick look over the crowd and spotted Cole standing up from a picnic table. He was there with Megan and their kids. I jumped to my feet and wiped the dirt from my hands onto my jeans as he came over to me.

"Whatcha doing here?" he asked, shaking my hand and patting me on the shoulder.

"Got an invite from a kid and his mother at the park yesterday," I replied. "What about you? I thought you went to Pines Baptist."

"We do go to Pines, but we are enrolling Justin into the pre-school here this coming school year. They invited us to come to the barbeque to get acquainted with some of the teachers and staff at the church." Cole looked past me and at Christopher. "Hi, Christopher."

"Hey, Mr. Taylor," he replied.

Cole smiled and directed his attention back to me. "So you guys went to a park yesterday?"

"Yeah, we did. Christopher is staying with me while Ems visits our mom. We ended up at the park because we lost power."

"Oh jeez! I heard about that outage on the news, it was pretty widespread. Thankfully we lived outside of the affected area," Cole replied. "So what were you doing in the park?"

"Playing baseball," I replied.

"Awesome. And that reminds me. The guys at the station want to get another game going in a week, if you are interested?"

"I'd love to play again. I found that bucket of balls in my garage by the way," I replied.

"So they were there? Not stolen from the kids you thought were playing in your garage?" Cole asked.

"Yeah they were there. He just didn't look behind a stack of newspapers," Christopher laughed.

Cole laughed and covered his mouth to try to hide it.

"Shut it," I replied, smiling. "Heard anything on my suspension?"

Cole stopped laughing and shook his head. "Jensen is pretty upset about it all. I'm trying to convince him to overlook the fight and stress the fact you were defending Gomer."

I nodded.

"You should try to talk to Foster about it... maybe apologize about his girlfriend and the whole Christmas party fiasco?"

My jaw clenched at the suggestion and Cole placed his hand on my shoulder.

"Put that pride aside. Your job is on the line," Cole said.

I nodded. "I'll think about it."

"How's your mom doing?" Cole asked.

I shrugged. "She's okay. Went and saw her like you suggested."

"Hey," Kristen said, interrupting us as she came around the side of the tree.

I turned and said, "Hey, Kristen."

She smiled as she came over to me. Just then, Megan called out for Cole to come back over to the picnic table to help with the boys.

"You know that man?" Kristen asked as Cole headed back to Megan.

"He's like a brother to me. Why?" I asked.

"That man saved my sister's life last year. She was stuck in a car and he helped her. After the accident, she found his picture in the newspaper preceding the funeral of the captain."

I nodded as I tried to recall car wrecks from the last year. "I have been on Cole's shift for a long time. What's her name?"

"Oh really? You're a firefighter too?" She asked.

"Yes, Ma'am," I replied with a grin.

"Maybe you were there with him that day? Her name is Monica," Kristen replied.

"Oh yeah..." I replied, recalling the accident down on Division street. "Did she make a full recovery? I remember we had to use the Jaws of Life on that car of hers."

"She did, yes. The car, not so much..."

I laughed. "Yeah, the Jaws of Life has a way of doing that."

Interrupting our conversation, a man got up near the front of the crowd. "I'm Pastor Tom and I'd like to welcome you out today. Hope you all are enjoying the beautiful weather." He paused waiting for the conversations to die down across the crowd. Kristen and I sat down by the tree. "We will be having a youth group football game of two hand touch after the barbeque, so all the youth just head over to the field after you finish up with your food. Let's bless the food and dig in!"

Everybody bowed their heads as a warm summer breeze blew in from the north and pushed a few strands of Kristen's blonde curly hair into my face. She grabbed the loose hair quickly and apologized in a whisper as she got it under control. But it was too late. Those strands carried a smell so wonderful, it'd made me forget about the world around me. I tried to focus on the pastor's prayer as he said it, but I kept thinking about Kristen. Why? I wondered. A smell? It didn't make any sense to me, but I could not get her off my mind through the entire prayer and then when everyone began to get food. We both stayed back at the tree and waited for the line to die down.

"Krissy," Tyson said upon approaching us with a plate of food. He handed her the plate. "I got those little tomatoes you like along with some fruit and cheese."

"Thank you, Tyson. That was sweet of you," she replied with a smile, taking the plate from his hands.

"I'm going to go get in line," I said, standing up. "Tyson," I said, greeting him with a nod as I walked past him and headed over to the tables that held the food.

Grabbing a paper plate and napkin from the table, I kept my eyes locked on Tyson and Kristen. Did they have something going on? I wondered. Then, I shook it off. It wasn't my business. I just played baseball with her son and smelled her hair, I wasn't in a position to question her relationship status.

"Burger or dog?" a woman with gloves asked with a friendly smile.

"Burger," I replied, looking past her at Tyson and Kristen again. I saw Tyson sit down next to her and I sighed.

"You okay, Sir?" the lady asked as she put the burger onto a bun and onto my plate.

I looked at her with a slight embarrassment that she noticed my sigh. Nodding, I replied, "Yeah,

I'm fine."

Continuing down the table, I filled my plate with chips, veggies and fruit. There wasn't much room for anything else. As I glanced over at the tree again, I noticed Tyson and Kristen were no longer there. Where'd they go? I wondered, looking over my shoulder across the crowd. I looked over to the football field and just saw a couple footballs sitting on the sidelines. No Kristen, no Tyson. They weren't anywhere in sight. They definitely have something going on, I thought to myself as I went over to the large trough of ice water. Reaching down, I grabbed a water bottle from beneath the surface. Shaking the excess water off of the bottle, I ventured back over to the tree with my plate of food.

After a few minutes, Kristen returned to the tree. Looking up at her, unable to say anything with a bite of burger in my mouth, I scooted over to make room for her. She had brought another plate of food over.

"Sorry about that," she said as she set her water down and began to eat her fruit salad.

I shook my head as I finished chewing. "It's no problem."

"Tyson just needed some help finding the footballs for the game."

I laughed as I took a bite of my watermelon.

"What?" she asked.

"Nothing," I replied.

"Seriously, what?" she pressed.

"You two obviously have something going on... you don't need to hide it with some fake story to me."

She set her fork down on her plate and raised an eyebrow. "Excuse me? There is nothing going on between Tyson and myself. I told you what happened because I am interested in you and didn't want you to *think* anything was going on there."

"Really? The footballs are already over there on the field."

She glanced over at the field and shook her head as she scoffed. "I guess that explains why we didn't find any... Ugh."

"What?"

"Tyson."

"What about him?"

"I think he just pulled me away to screw with your head... he's had a thing for me for quite some time now..."

"Why would you go with him if that's the case?" I asked.

She took another bite of her fruit salad and tilted her head back and forth waiting to finish the bite before speaking. "I can't help but think the best of people... I honestly didn't think he had ill intentions with it until now."

"I see," I replied. I grabbed a potato chip from my plate and popped it into my mouth as I spotted Tyson over talking to a couple of people by the dessert table. He made eye contact with me and gave me a nod before returning to his conversation. Did the guy really feel that threatened by me? I wondered.

Kristen's phone rang. Putting her plate down, she checked the caller ID. "Ugh... its work." She stood up and walked around the pine tree and out of sight.

"Hey, Uncle Kane," Christopher said, coming over to me.

"Yeah?" I replied, finishing the last chip on my plate.

"Blake and the other guys are heading over to the LAN party after the football game... and they wanted to see if I could go and stay the night?"

I smiled up at him and handed him my plate. "Sure, but I need you to toss that in the trash."

"Okay, awesome!" Christopher replied, taking the plate.

"Wait... what time are you going to be back at my place tomorrow? Or do you need a ride?"

Christopher looked over at Blake and the other kids with him.

One kid stepped forward and said, "I'm sure my dad can drive him to your place. Like around lunch time or something?"

I nodded. "Sounds good to me."

"Sweet. Thanks, Uncle Kane," Christopher said as Kristen came back around the tree. Christopher and the other boys headed towards the football field.

"Man, don't you ever wish you could go live off the land and live in a hut somewhere off the grid?" Kristen asked as she sat back down next to her plate of fruit salad.

I laughed. "Off the grid? I like being on the grid... I'd go nuts without a sense of connection to everybody else."

She nodded. "That's true... and I'd hate not

having any of the luxuries we have in the city."

I nodded in agreement. "What makes you say that to begin with?" I asked, leaning back on my hands as I rested in a comfortable position with my feet kicked out in front.

"Work. We just got hit with a health inspection and if we don't comply within a week to these crazy requests, they'll shut us down."

"That's rough... Where do you work?"

"Stix. It's a restaurant-"

"On Nevada Street," I finished her sentence.

"Yeah," she grinned. "You know about Stix? Most people I tell about it haven't ever heard of it or been there. It's fairly new... just been open under a year."

"I've eaten there. It's good. My favorite thing I had was those little warm donuts with the different dipping sauces... chocolate, white..."

Kristen laughed and covered her mouth as she threw her head back. "Sorry, I just can't help but laugh."

"Why?" I asked, leaning in smiling.

"Those are *always* what people order when

they come in. My boss hates it. He has all this fancy duck and steak on the menu and people come back for the donuts every single time."

I smiled. "They are delicious."

She nodded. "They are pretty good. And I love my job... it's just hard sometimes being part of management."

"I'm sure it is."

"I just got promoted at the beginning of the year after one of the previous assistant managers moved back to California. Since that happened, it feels like I have no time at all. The good news is I do have a vacation coming up shortly."

Nodding, I looked over at Blake as he was talking to Christopher. "Have you seen an impact on Blake since you took the promotion?"

"Yeah." She looked over at him. "He seems more distant. That's why I try to keep him busy with the church and whatnot... I don't want him to end up getting into trouble."

"Yeah, it's a crucial age."

She nodded. "It really is."

All the parents began getting up and gravitating towards the garbage cans to dump their plates and head over to the football field. We both stood up and joined the movement over to watch the game. On the way over, Tyson jogged up to my side.

"Hey, a few of us older guys are going to toss the old pigskin around on Sunday after church... you want to join us?"

I shook my head. "I don't know..."

Cole overheard us. "I'll go if you go," he said from behind us. I looked over my shoulder.

"Alright, I'm game," I said, nodding.

"Awesome... games at 1pm just out here on the football field after service."

"Right on," I replied as I watched Tyson jog further into the crowd to tell the other guys about it.

"He's a good guy, try not to take it too personal," Kristen said.

I nodded. "Yeah, seems real nice," I replied half-heartedly.

The rest of the afternoon and partway into the evening seemed to fly by as all the parents lined the bleachers to watch the football game. Sitting with Cole and a few of the other men from the church in the bleachers, I learned of a men's retreat that was coming up in the fall. I wasn't sure if I'd end up attending, but it sounded interesting. It was a multi-church retreat up to a place outside of Spokane called Suncrest. In big bold letters across the top, the little pamphlet Cole gave me said: **A weekend full of promise**. I put the pamphlet in my back pocket and pushed it out of my mind.

After the game and on the way out to my car in the parking lot, I saw Christopher getting in a car with Blake and some of the other youth. Shooting a wave over to them, I smiled when he waved back. Christopher might be mixed up with some bad kids like Kegan, but he had a good heart, I thought to myself as I got in my car.

CHAPTER 6

Rising early the next day, I found the quietness in the apartment refreshing after the last couple days with Christopher around. I loved the kid dearly, but I also appreciated my own space and life. After putting on a pot of coffee in the kitchen, I headed outside to figure out exactly where the leak in my garage roof was. I could have called the landlord, but I'd spent my fair share of time on rooftops back in the summer before my senior year of high school, and I felt confident in my own abilities. As I was setting up the ladder against the garage downstairs from my apartment, my phone buzzed in my pocket. Slipping it out, I saw it was Emily.

"Hello?" I answered as I held onto the top of the ladder.

"Hey, how's Christopher?" she asked.

"He's doing good. He's with some of the youth from Valley Baptist at something called a 'LAN party.'"

"A what party? You let him go partying?"

Man, she was dumb, I thought before I responded. "No, Emily. It's like with video games... and I said from Valley Baptist... you know, a church? Anyways... why? What's up?"

"Okay... I'm on the way back from mom's right now. She's getting worse, Kane. She's getting weaker... I don't know if it'll even be months."

I glared out over my garage and towards the park just over my complex's chain-linked fence. I could feel fear and worry rise inside of me. With tears welling in my eyes, I cleared my throat and said, "I want to go see her."

"That's also why I was calling. I think you should go see her... I don't know how much longer she has."

"Stop saying that Ems... you're worrying yourself too much. I'll go see her." Glancing at my phone, I saw it was still relatively early. Nine o'clock. "Dang it. Christopher isn't here yet... he won't be here until about noon."

"Well, I can call him and just go pick him up from wherever he is at."

I didn't think it was a very good idea. Christopher needed those Christian boys' influence as much as possible right now. But knowing my sister was very anti-God, I couldn't let her in onto that fact. So I said it in a way that made sense for her. "He's having fun... just let him be over there."

"Okay, well... I don't want him at your house alone."

"Yeah, just come over here and hang out until he gets dropped off."

"Alright," she replied. "I'll talk to you later."

"Sounds good."

I hung up with my sister and looked across the roof from atop the ladder. I figured I would at least try to see if I could find the leak before I left to my mom's house. Scanning the shingles, I couldn't spot any real issues with my naked eye. Climbing up onto the roof, I began walking in search of any damage I could spot. Coming over to the valley, the spot where my garage intersects with my neighbor's garage, I noticed something amiss. The shingles in the valley were overlapped improperly. Dropping a knee down, I inspected. Sure enough, it was backwards. The water had been running directly down the shingle and straight into my garage. My attic must have been catching the run off.

As I returned to my ladder, I called my landlord and let him know about the issue. I offered him to let me charge the supplies and labor against the cost of my rent if I was willing to fix it. He said he had a guy that could do it, so he'd send him over to fix it sometime in the coming week.

On my way back up to my apartment to grab my keys, my phone buzzed in my pocket. I bet it's Christopher, I thought to myself. Pulling out my phone, I saw it was the Chief.

"Hello?" I answered partially excited, partially scared.

"McCormick," Chief Jensen replied. "I want to let you know that you are free to return to work in the morning."

"Yes!" I shouted as I jumped a little as I made my way up to my apartment.

"Don't get too excited yet, McCormick. This

is just temporary while we continue the investigation. Foster was in my office this morning and he was calling for you to get fired. I was able to pull a few strings on the fact he was upset with you and the police Chief and I both agreed he had some vendetta against you. You need to keep yourself out of hot water. For good this time."

I nodded as I said, "I don't even drink anymore, Sir."

"Whatever. Just keep straight and narrow with your duties around the station and keep your cool off the clock."

"Okay. Thanks!" I said.

"You're welcome. Have a good rest of your day. We'll see you in the morning."

"Yes, sir!"

I hurried into my apartment and called Cole immediately.

"Dude, I'm back tomorrow!" I said.

"I heard. That's great, McCormick."

"I know, right?" I asked as I grabbed my keys off the counter. "Thank you for all your help in this, Taylor."

"You're welcome." I could hear his boys getting upset in the background. "I gotta go, but I'll see you in the morning."

"Alright, take it easy."

My sister showed up as I hung up with Cole. Opening the door, she came inside. "Hey," I said, greeting her.

She went into the kitchen and poured a cup of coffee. She looked stressed. Opening the fridge, she looked around for something inside before looking over at me, "No creamer?"

"Top shelf, in the back. It's behind the Soy milk," I replied.

"Great," she replied with a heavy sigh.

"Calm down, Sis," I said.

She scoffed and turned to me. "Try telling me that after you see her." She looked back into the fridge and snagged the creamer from the shelf. As she poured the creamer into the coffee, she looked over at me, "Stop standing there looking at me like that... I'm fine. Go see mom, Dude!"

"Alright, alright," I said, raising my hands up as I backed my way up to the door. Grabbing my shades off the end table near the door, I put them on and headed down to the parking lot.

As I pulled into the driveway at my mother's house, I immediately got a bad feeling in the pit of my stomach. The way my sister was talking, I didn't know what to expect even though I was just up at her house a few days back. But when my mom didn't step outside to greet me like every other time I had visited over the years, I began to worry. Looking through the windshield, I saw the screen door flap in the wind like something out of a horror movie.

"This can't be good," I said, as I turned off my car. Getting out, I walked the gravel up to the front door. Knocking lightly, I said, "Mom?" I glanced into the living room window and didn't see her on the couch. Turning the doorknob, I stepped into the house, not knowing what to expect.

Seeing the back sliding glass door open, I spotted her sitting outside on the back porch. I felt relieved as I walked through the house and approached her.

"Mom!" I said, as I walked past her down the steps and turned around to her. "Are you okay? I was scared to death."

She set her cup of tea down and stood up to hug me. "Of course, I'm okay, Kane!" she said with a grin.

"You didn't hear the door? I was knocking," I replied as we embraced.

She shook her head as she sat back down. Picking up her tea she took a sip and said, "Not at all. I just came outside a few minutes ago because Roofus was getting restless. I wasn't able to play fetch with him the last couple days your sister had been here. She'd only take him for a walk! And wouldn't let me go outside at all."

I laughed.

"Don't you laugh!" she said with a laugh in her tone. "Your sister kept me cooped up in the house." She paused. "She means well, but dang it! I need to be able to move around and breathe!"

"I agree with you, Mom. Emily is way too strict with you and freaked out about all this..."

"Son?" she asked, quieting her voice.

"Yeah?"

She set her tea down again and reached out her weathered and aging hands to grasp onto one of my hands. Holding it close to her chest, she said, "Would you take me up the mountain? The one we used to walk up when you and Emily were just a couple of kiddos?"

I recalled our day hikes with picnic lunches as I looked out over the forest covered land towards the mountain in the distance and replied, "I know what mountain you're talking about, but I don't think walking that many miles would be a good idea in your condition, Mom...."

She laughed. "I meant to just take me to the summit. We can go park off Tod Road, that will cut quite a bit of time off the trip." I knew exactly where she was talking about. It was a patch of dirt off to the side of the mountain road that had the perfect walking trail up to the summit.

I mulled it over in my mind for a moment before making eye contact with her. Her ocean blue eyes had so much hope in them, I couldn't possibly turn down the idea. "Okay, let's do it."

We got into my car and hightailed it over to Tod road which took about fifteen minutes by car. As I got out and shut my door, a flood of pleasant memories rushed through my mind as I saw the tree in which we carved our names into so many years ago. The smell of the pine trees filled my nose and the quietness of the still forest brought a smile to my face. Suddenly I heard my mother trying to open her own door by herself. I hurried around the car to go assist her.

"Jeez, Mom... You should have waited for me to help."

"You look like you were having a seizure judging by that blank stare over there."

"What?" I asked, confused.

"Whenever someone just stares blankly like you were doing... it's a seizure. Doctor Ricardo told me that years ago."

I laughed. "Whatever, Mom. I was just reflecting." I gently grabbed her arm and helped her the rest of the way out of the car. Looking up the trail that was before us, I smiled thinking back to Emily and I racing up to the first fork in the path. "This place brings back so many memories," I said.

She smiled as she intertwined her arm with mine. "I know... I love it. You know you kids were so good for me when you were little... if I didn't get blessed with well-behaved children, I don't know what I would have done. Your father, even when we were still together, was always gone off out of the country and traveling."

I nodded as we continued up the path. "You were always an amazing mother to us. If there was an award for 'best mom,' you would have gotten it."

She scoffed as she turned and looked into the woods. "I don't know about that, Son."

"Well, in our eyes you have been nothing but amazing."

She smiled softly and tightened her hold onto my arm as we ventured up a steep incline in the path. We walked for a bit until my mom became tired and sat down on a log that lay next to the path. I joined her on the log as she looked around at all the trees that surrounded us. She said, "Isn't it amazing?"

I looked up and around. "It's pretty cool up here."

"God designed all of this, Kane."

I nodded.

"My hope is you know where I'm going after this old body finally kicks the bucket." She patted my leg. "I'm going to be with Jesus and your brother Kyle."

"I know..." I replied softly.

"You seem conflicted," she replied.

"I just don't get it all..." I said. "It's hard for me to wrap my mind around the concept of God at times. We have billions of stars, unknown amounts of galaxies... yet the Earth is the center of it all? It's all out there because of Earth? Because of us?"

She smiled and looked to the tops of the trees. "God created this earth. Created light. Created everything, dearest Son. And I think it's possible that all those galaxies and space out there was a result of God's creation. He spoke everything into existence and what we know about speech, we know there is sometimes an echo. So basically, all that other stuff out there would be just an echo through eternity of His original creation."

I smiled. "You're such a deep thinker, Mom."

She nodded. "Everything has its purpose, Son. You have to know that."

I shook my head. "There's no purpose in death. There was no reason why Kyle had to die over in Iraq or that you had to get cancer."

She shrugged. "I don't believe God causes bad things to happen. He cannot sin and He's not the author of it. However, I do believe God can work the most pitiful situations into something beautiful. God trades our ashes for beauty, and our pain for joy."

"But how do you know you're right about everything?" I asked. "I just need something solid."

She laughed a little as she stood up. "You have to have faith, Kane. And faith is felt with the fingertips of your soul."

"I love you," I said, smiling, rising to my feet and pulling her up.

"I love you too, Son," she said as she kissed my cheek. Latching back onto my arm, she looked forward down the path, and I began leading her further up the trail to the summit of the mountain.

CHAPTER 7

Ted and Micah were in the multi-purpose room upstairs at the fire station the next day when I arrived. Walking in, they both looked over their shoulders at me and nodded.

"You're back already?" Ted asked as he looked back at the television set.

"Yeah, the investigation is still on-going, but the Chief told me I could come back," I replied.

"Did you get those new rims on your ride

yet?" Micah asked, getting up from the couch as he came over to me. Micah loved my car more than any of the other guys at the station. He even went with me to pick it up in Oregon back seven months ago.

"Oh, yeah, man! I forgot to tell you the other day. You want to come check them out?" I asked.

Micah glanced over at the clock on the wall. "Yeah, I have some time.

On the way out to the parking lot, he asked, "How's your mom doing?"

"She's good," I replied. "Just got back from seeing her last night. Went up there for the day." Going out the side door to the parking lot, I held open the door for Micah.

"That's good."

"Yeah. I'm hopeful she'll be around for a while," I replied as we came out to my car.

"I'm sure she will be. Oh, wow, those are some nice rims, McCormick!" Micah said as he bent down.

"I'm glad someone appreciates them. They were a fortune."

Micah nodded as he rose back up to his feet. "Hey –Taylor tells me you were with a girl at the barbeque?"

"Kristen. Yeah, she's cool."

"You need to be careful, McCormick. This gal isn't like Ashley. She has a kid."

I felt offended at his statement. "What do you mean?" I retorted. "First off, we're just friends. Second off, I'm good with kids."

Raising a hand up, Micah replied, "Woah, Kane. I'm not trying to upset you. I'm trying to warn you. A lot comes with a relationship with a woman who has a kid. They aren't like the single ladies you are accustomed to."

Without another word, I headed back inside, shutting the door forcefully behind me as I came back into the fire station. I went into the kitchen and grabbed a coffee cup out of the cupboard.

"Morning," Cole said, startling me as he walked into the kitchen.

Jumping a little, I turned around. "Oh, hey," I replied quickly as I poured myself a cup of coffee.

"What's wrong?" he asked. "You seem on edge."

Looking over at him, I glared and then went over to the kitchen doorway to check down the hall.

Micah wasn't there. Turning back to Cole, I said, "It's Freeman. He thinks he needs to lecture me about Kristen. We're not even together. We're barely friends."

Cole looked down as he replied, "Sorry about that, it's my fault." He looked up at me as I walked past him to get my coffee. "I mentioned you were with her at the barbeque."

"Why would you even tell him that?" I asked.

Cole shrugged as he got a coffee cup. "Just came up while we were talking about the barbeque. He knows Justin's starting pre-school there soon."

"Well, if you could not talk about me with the other guys, that'd be great," I said sharply.

Cole laughed. "What?"

"I don't appreciate it," I replied as I left the kitchen without another word.

Cole followed me as I walked into the dining hall and put his hand on my shoulder, stopping me in my footsteps. I turned around and asked, "What, Taylor?"

"You didn't appreciate it when I gave you the cold shoulder when I was going through that stuff with Megan."

"Yeah, so?" I replied.

"Don't shut me out or the other guys here because you don't want to deal with what's going on in your life. This isn't high school, McCormick. We're like brothers here, and that bond we have is forged by the fires we fight. We don't need drama. Freeman was trying to help you and you know that."

"You don't even know what was said," I retorted.

"What was it he said?"

"He told me she had a kid and she's not like the single ladies I'm used to seeing."

Cole shrugged. "Yeah?"

"I don't need that..."

"Sorry, bud. This is an overreaction on your part. Micah knows you are used to a different type of woman. And guess what? Kristen is going to pick her kid over you every opportunity that comes up. It's not a relationship with just her. It's her and the kid."

I nodded. Cole was right. I had overreacted. Micah was just trying to help. "I'm not anything but friends with her, but you're right. I'll go talk to Micah."

Cole took a sip of his coffee and nodded.

Leaving the dining hall, I went to go find Micah. He was sitting on the steps that led down to the bay area of the fire station.

"Hey," I said, sitting down next to him.

"McCormick," Micah said, looking over at me for a moment.

"I know you were just trying to help... I'm sorry for reacting the way I did."

He nodded. "Thanks. But I think I might have jumped the gun a little bit. You're like a son to me, and I was just trying to warn you based on the assumption you were dating that girl. That was my bad. I'm sorry."

"I get it. Thanks for caring, man."

"We cool?" Micah asked.

"We're cool," I replied.

A call came in just as we were finishing up our lunch later that day. It was a call for a two-story house fire at the corner of Oak and Shannon. Without hesitation, we all rose to our feet and rushed out of the dining hall and down the hallway to the fire pole.

One by one, we slid down the pole and got into our turnouts. My heart raced and adrenaline shot through me as I suited up. Cole came up to me and patted me on the shoulder.

"You ready to roll again?" he asked.

"Absolutely," I replied with a quick and confident tone.

"Keep your head in the game out there," Cole said as he climbed up into the passenger seat in the front of the ladder truck.

"Will do."

I finished getting my gear on and climbed into the back seat next to Brian. Glancing over at Brian, I could see something was off and as we rolled out of the bay area, I asked, "What's got you all upset, Gomer?"

"Nothing," he retorted.

Cole laughed from the front seat as he paused from looking at his laptop to turn around to us. "Gomer, you know my four year old acts like that when he's upset? All he says is 'Nuffin.' "

Micah began laughing as he turned out of the station. "You're still the Rookie, we'll get rid of you if we need to," Micah said, jokingly.

"Shut it, Freeman," Brian replied.

"Hey!" Cole snapped at Brian. "You got a problem, you need to speak up."

I wondered if it had something to do about me not drinking anymore. We weren't really talking much since I left that night at the bar. "Is this because I'm not going out with you anymore?" I asked.

Brain shook his head. "Nah man... trouble with the old lady."

"Well, if you would move out you wouldn't have a problem with your mom anymore, Gomer," Cole replied with a chuckle.

"You reading any of that Bible Study I gave you?" Micah asked as he turned onto Shannon Street.

"I've glanced at it..." Brian replied, turning his eyes to his window.

"You gotta work on your relationship with God," Cole said with a nod to Brian. "And move out."

Brian replied, "I don't know if she's ready to

be on her own again. She struggles with getting around the house."

"You're already gone from the house for twenty-four hour blocks of time," I said.

Suddenly Micah slammed on the breaks, quickly bringing us to a stop.

"What was that for?" I shouted up to Micah.

"There is a person in the street!" he snapped back as he reached for his door. We all jumped out of the truck and ran to the front to see that a woman was lying on the pavement.

"Did we hit her?" Gomer asked.

"Of course not! I stopped before we ran her over," Micah replied.

Looking up from the woman in the road, I could see the house fire a couple of homes up ahead. I ran over to the sidewalk and hurried my steps up to the scene.

Finding a young teenage boy standing out by the mailbox, I approached him as I kept looking over at the house that was burning. "Are there any people inside?" I asked.

He had a blank stare as he turned his head to look over at me. "My Grandma. She's still in there..."

"And who is the woman back there in the street?" I asked, pointing back to where the rest of the guys were and the trucks.

"That was the neighbor. She tried to go in and save my grandma, but couldn't do it."

Looking over at the house, I saw the flames growing rapidly. "Okay," I replied. "I'm going to grab my gear really fast and then go in."

He nodded and turned back to the house. He pulled out his cell phone from his pocket and began taking a picture. What is wrong with kids these days? I wondered as I jogged back to the truck. The ambulance had arrived and began moving the wounded woman from the street onto a stretcher as I came up to the side of the truck. Opening up the side, I grabbed my equipment. Cole asked, "What's going on?"

"There's a woman inside, I'm going in."

He nodded. "Okay. We'll be right behind you."

Returning to the house, I walked past the teenager and asked, "Where inside is your grandma?"

"She's near the back side of the house. In the spare bedroom by the kitchen."

Getting up to the house, I peered in through the open doorway. It wasn't heavily saturated with smoke inside, making it easier on me for visibility. I was able to see through the living room and spotted the kitchen off to the far left. The fire looked to be originating from the kitchen area. Walking through the living room, I could see family pictures in plastic frames melting and being destroyed with every passing moment. Getting to the back room where the boy said she was, I kicked open the door and found the grandmother on the bed.

"Ma'am!" I shouted as I rushed over to the bed.

She wasn't alert or coming conscious. I shook her and shouted again, "Ma'am!"

There was no response. The flames reached the doorway behind and started wrapping themselves into the room, blocking my exit. Looking around, I spotted a window just on the other side of the bed. I leaped onto the bed and ran over to it. Using my fist, I busted out the glass. I grabbed bedding and placed it over the broken shards of glass that remained in the window. Pausing, I got on the radio.

"Taylor. I'm on the north side window. Coming out in just a moment with a unconscious woman."

"Copy that," he replied.

Taking a deep breath, I bent down and began pulling the woman over to the window. As I inched her across the bed towards the window, Brian climbed through and helped me get her the rest of the way out. As we brought her out, Brian leaped down first and with the help of Cole, pulled her from the window.

Cole got on his radio. "I need a medic on the north side of the structure."

As we pulled her away from the burning building and into the grass, the paramedics came around the side of the house with the grandson by their side.

"Is she going to be okay?" the teenager boy asked me as he ran to her and dropped to his knees.

I nodded. "She'll be alright."

The paramedics huddled around her as they checked for vitals and one of them put an oxygen mask over her face. Watching as they loaded her on the gurney, I saw the boy crying as he held her hand and I thought of my mother. Reality kicked me in the side of the head right in that moment.

"You alright?" Cole asked, putting his hand on my shoulder as I stared blankly at the teenage boy and his grandmother.

"I'm heading up front to help with the frontal attack on the fire," Brian said to the two of us before jetting off.

We both nodded to him.

As Brian rounded the corner, I said to Cole, "That kid was broken up about his grandma... and she's probably going to be okay. My mom's going to be dead soon... just kind of hit me."

Cole patted my shoulder and said, "Don't focus on that bad part, man. Just enjoy the time you have left with her and celebrate her life."

I nodded as we began walking back to the front of the house.

Back at the fire station, Cole was sitting at the table reading the newspaper as I walked into the kitchen to grab a cup of coffee. As I walked past him, he set the paper down and asked, "Any updates on your mom?"

After I poured my cup of coffee, I joined him

at the table in the dining hall. "She seemed fine yesterday when I was there."

"Nothing too concerning?" Cole asked.

I shook my head. "No, but Emily sure thinks she's about to kick the bucket."

"Why?" he asked.

I shrugged. "I don't know... but that's why I went up there yesterday. Emily made it sound pretty imminent."

"Well, I know in the final months of my father's life, I saw him whenever I could. Every minute that passes is a moment lost."

"Yeah. I know I got freaked out at the fire... but for the most part it just doesn't feel real to me..." I shook my head. "My mom won't be here in a couple months probably. That statement sounds weird and foreign. But the truth is, I could get a phone call today saying she's gone... I don't know how to process that."

"I understand. Even after my dad died, I couldn't wrap my head around it all. It's not until I saw his empty chair sitting in the living room that it really began to get real. And you honestly don't ever get used to someone not being around, you just learn to live without them..." Shaking his head as he paused, he continued, "But, you shouldn't focus on that. Focus on the time you have left with her. Like I said before."

I nodded. "I agree."

Our conversation got quiet as we both stared at the table. Then, Cole suddenly asked, "So are you going to start attending Valley Baptist regularly?"

"I'll see how I like it on Sunday. I don't know, though."

"Yeah... Can I ask you something?" Cole asked.

I looked at him with one eyebrow lowered. "Not if you preface it with that."

He smiled. "It's not bad, just serious."

"Sure."

"Do you believe?"

I adjusted in my seat. "What do you mean? In what? ...Like God? Yeah."

"Do you believe in the death, burial and resurrection of Jesus Christ?"

"Sure do," I replied.

"Then..." Cole paused. "Never mind," he said,

waving a hand.

"Wait a second," I said, sitting up more in my seat and leaning in. "You can't do that. What were you going to say?"

Cole sighed. "Nothing, don't worry about it."

Shaking my head, I said, "Out with it, Taylor."

He looked nervous as he continued, "Okay. What are you doing?"

I looked around and laughed. "What?"

"If you believe, why aren't you in church? If you believe, why are you living like you got it all handled without God?"

Who did this guy think he was? I wondered. My anger began to warm. "Wow..."

Cole sat back and said, "I'm just curious."

I shook my head and scoffed. "This is coming from the guy who couldn't get it figured out with his wife and almost lost everything."

"Yeah. Exactly," he replied. "I spent a lot of time not relying on God and got nowhere." My anger was just about to consume me, it was burning hot.

I shrugged. "I guess I just don't feel like I

need God's help a whole lot."

"Your mother is dying-"

His comment set my anger a blaze, causing me to lunge across the table, tackling Cole backwards and onto the floor. I slugged him in the face. Raising my fist to punch him again, I was interrupted by a shout that came from the other side of the room.

"McCormick!" Brian shouted.

Stopping, I stood up and looked over at him. Looking back at Cole, I saw the disappointment in his eyes as he began to stand up. He wiped the blood from his lip. Micah came inside from the balcony. Ted and Rick came in from the other room. Each one of them looked at me like I was a stranger. I ducked my head and hurried my steps past Brian and down the hallway to the stairwell to leave.

CHAPTER 8

On the drive home, I felt sick to my stomach. I had been in fights before, but never like this. Not at work. I betrayed my brotherhood and their trust. How am I ever going to show my face there again? Slamming the steering wheel I screamed in frustration. Why'd Cole have to set me off like that? I wondered as I squealed my wheels around a corner on the way back to my apartment. As I came up the street I saw a woman walking down the sidewalk. As I got closer, I realized it was Kristen, and my frustration over Cole took a backseat in my mind.

Slowing down, I rolled my window down and asked, "What are you doing out here walking?"

She looked over at me and furrowed her eyebrows. "Car troubles. Don't worry about it." Her short and agitated tone led me to believe I had done something wrong, but I didn't pry in the moment.

"Hop in. I'll give you a ride."

"No thanks," she replied.

I pulled a u-turn and came right up to her side as she continued walking. "Did I do something to offend you?" I asked, lifting my shades up and setting them on my head.

She stopped and looked at me. "You're a phony and I don't like fake people." She looked forward and kept walking. I pulled the car over to the side of the road, and caught up to her on the sidewalk by foot.

"Kristen. What are you talking about?" I asked, gently touching her arm to get her to stop.

She swatted my hand away and kept walking.

"C'mon!" I shouted. "I deserve some kind of idea of what I did so wrong."

She stopped and turned back to face me on the sidewalk. She speedily walked back up to me and got within a few inches of my face. "I know all about you, Kane McCormick. Or should I say Mr. November." Her words confused me for only a moment and as it sank in, I knew what she was referring to. I had posed for a firefighter calendar four years ago and she must have seen it.

"Where'd you see the calendar?" I asked.

"Does it matter?" she snapped. "I didn't see it. Your sister told me all about you." She turned and kept walking down the street.

"My sister? When did you even see her?" I asked. She kept walking without a response. I didn't appreciate my sister divulging my personal history to her, but Kristen had no right to judge me. "Whatever," I laughed. "I guess I can't be better than my past..." I said, shaking my head as I turned and headed back to my car.

Getting back to my apartment, I slammed the door behind me. Cole and now Emily? Who else could betray me today? I pulled my phone out and called Emily.

"Hello?"

"Hey," I said sharply. "Could we chat? You at work?"

"You sound upset..."

I shook my phone and squeezed it screaming silently. It took everything in me to control myself as I brought it back up to my ear. "*I am* upset... You talked to Kristen?"

She was silent for a moment and then said, "Come to my work. Meet me in the courtyard out front."

"Okay. Be there in an hour. I need to shower."

I hung up the phone and headed for the bathroom.

When I arrived to the hospital an hour later, I saw her sitting on the white stone bench in the courtyard out front. After parking, I got out and put my shades on top of my head as I slammed the door.

"Kane..." she said softly with tears in her eyes as she rose to her feet. Her hands were clasped together and she had her doctor's coat on.

"How dare you, Ems!" I shouted as I approached her through the grass.

"You don't understand," she pleaded as she rose a hand and held it out.

Scoffing, I shook my head. "You don't get it. That girl doesn't know anything about me and you just gave her my whole past."

"Kane," Emily said softly.

"No. I'm sick of you thinking you know everything! I was at Mom's yesterday, she was fine. I took her up on the old trail up along the mountain. She loved it."

"Kane." She grabbed onto my arm and I swatted it away.

"You know what, Emily? This whole thing," I said, pointing back to the hospital. "Has gotten up in your head and you think you're God because you walk around with that white coat."

She shook her head as she began crying.

"Go ahead, turn on the water works, I don't care, Ems. You seriously need to get over yourself."

"Mom's dead," she said bluntly, looking up at me with red, swollen eyes.

"What? No. I just saw her," I retorted, relaxing my posture as confusion began to cloud my train of thought.

She came closer to me, touching my arm again. This time I didn't swat it away. "I just saw her twenty minutes ago, Kane, before she passed. She was life flighted from Colville."

My lips perched together creating a thin line. Fighting back my tears I shook my head. "No... That's not true. I'd know if mom was dead."

She erupted in tears again and clung onto me. Crying into my chest, she said, "I didn't have time to call you... it all happened so quickly."

Tears trickled down my cheeks as I wrapped my arms around my sister. "This was my fault..." I said, letting go of Emily.

She shook her head and said, "No, Kane. It was just her time to go."

"But I took her hiking..."

"It wasn't that."

I turned and began walking away from Emily.

"Kane, where are you going?" she yelled as she stayed behind at the white bench in the courtyard.

"I don't know..." I replied as I lowered my shades over my eyes. My chest felt as if it were collapsing into itself from the pain of never seeing my mother again.

Getting into my car, I didn't even look the direction of Emily in the courtyard. I just turned the key over and peeled out of the hospital parking lot.

I drove to a nearby liquor store and then headed north towards Colville. Inside some sort of weird daze, I felt no meaning to my existence. My mother had died, my job was most likely gone and the one girl I had partially been interested in loathed me. All within a few hours of each other. When it rains, it pours, I thought to myself as I mulled over the events.

Twenty minutes outside of Colville, I began to lay my foot on the gas pedal. The speed made me feel fear as I topped over a hundred miles an hour, and it gave me a shot of adrenaline. Suddenly, my phone rang. It was Jensen. I didn't care, I grabbed my phone and turned it off. Tossing the phone in the back seat, I reached over into the passenger seat of my car and grabbed the bottle of whiskey I picked up at the liquor store. I needed to fix this pain that was wedging itself into my existence. Whiskey was a quick solution to the problem. Coming up on my exit towards my mom's house, I saw cop lights up ahead, which caused me to slow down. No way was I going to jail.

Arriving at my mother's, I saw Roofus outside lying on the front porch. I parked my car and stumbled up to him. Looking down at Roofus, I tilted my head back and took a swig of the bottle in my hand. Setting the bottle of whiskey down on the porch, I laid down next to Roofus and began to pet him. "You missin' momma, aren't ya?" I asked.

He said nothing in reply.

Sighing, I stood back up and picked up my bottle. Looking at the front door, I hated she wasn't on the other side. No chocolate milk, no coffee, just an empty house full of memories. Opening the door, I let it swing freely open. All the smells of her remained, forcing memories to push against my mind and sorrows to fill my heart. The whiskey wasn't doing a very good job at managing the pain. Looking back at Roofus out on the steps, I said, "Come on in." Roofus and I went inside to the living room and I took a seat on the couch. I let a long, drawn out sigh come out of me as I relaxed and Roofus curled up on the floor near my feet.

Closing my eyes, I could feel my mom sitting in her chair just a few paces away from me. I smiled and then opened my eyes. The chair was empty and my smile fell away with the realization that only in my dreams would I be able to see her. She's really gone, I thought to myself as I took another drink from the bottle.

Looking down at Roofus, I asked him, "Why don't dogs cry?"

He didn't respond.

"Hmmm... Not much for words, are ya, boy?" Standing up, I went back to the front door to leave and noticed Roofus tailing right behind me. I nodded to him and grabbed the leash that hung on the wall near the front door. Bending a knee, I said, "You don't want to stay here alone here, do you?" I latched the leash to his collar and led him out the front door. Walking down the front steps of my mother's house, I looked towards the mountain and thought of our walk we had just went on the other day. It was the last thing I ever had done with her. Shaking my head, I continued on my way out to my car.

Putting Roofus in the back seat, I told him, "Don't you dare ruin that leather back there." Putting the driver's seat back into position, I climbed in and shut the door. Adjusting my mirror, I looked Roofus in the eyes. "You have to be my best friend now. And that means I'm going to trust you not to pee, poop or do anything else when you are in my car."

He yawned and made a strange sound. Suddenly a whiff of dog smell filled my nose and I shook my head at the smell. Disgusting, I thought.

I put the car in reverse and left my mom's house. Heading down the road, I saw the turn off for Tod Road. I took the turn off.

Stepping out of the car, I grabbed Roofus' leash and got him out of the back. I glanced over to where the trail started. I began walking through the gravel towards the entrance. Pausing my steps at the tree with all four of our names engraved, I reached up and ran my fingers over the grooves and thought back to that day we marked the tree.

Kyle was a teenager and overly excited by the pocket knife that our neighbor got him for his birthday the day of our walk. He begged mom the entire walk to be able to engrave one of the trees. She finally gave in, but it wasn't until we came back down the trail and we were at the last tree. He was so excited she said yes, that he jumped up about a foot in the air and landed funny when he came back down, spraining his ankle. He had to limp over to the tree to do the carving.

Roofus jerked on the leash, breaking me from my memory. We continued on our way up the trail for a few minutes until Roofus felt the need to pull me off the path. "C'mon!" I shouted as I tried yanking him back onto the trail. When he began to squat, I realized he needed to do some business. Turning around so I didn't face him, I said jokingly, "You could have done this before we left."

A lady and her daughter walked passed me on the trail as I was still waiting on Roofus.

"Hi," the little girl that couldn't have been more than six years old said.

I hid the bottle of whiskey behind my back and nodded. "Hi."

The two looked at me strangely as they continued on the path. I laughed a little and looked over my shoulder to see Roofus trying to cover up his business with dirt. The ground wasn't soft enough and the result was rather ineffective. "Enough of that," I said, pulling on the leash to lead him away and back to the trail.

As we walked, I looked up at the sunshine that was shining through the tops of the trees and wondered how God could do this to me and my sister. My mother was a devout Christian. She didn't need to die.

Finding a place to stop and rest, I sat down on the log that my mother sat on less than twenty-four hours ago. Shaking my head as I looked down at the grass and dirt between my feet, I began falling asleep. The heartache and turmoil inside of me was dulled to a small roar. The liquor had fulfilled its purpose. Suddenly, Roofus barked, startling me back awake.

I jumped up from my seat and looked around. There was nothing. Just Roofus, an empty forest and me. As Roofus and I began to continue on the path, something further up the trail caught a ray of sunshine beaming down through the trees and reflected a bright light. Almost immediately I grinned as I thought God had sent me some sort of sign. I darted up the trail and climbed over logs and bushes to get to the mysterious item. Coming to the item, I bent down on both my knees. Roofus was right there by my side, sniffing and doing his own investigation. I sighed with disappointment as the item was merely just a wrapper. I grabbed it and shoved it into my pocket as I stood up. "People shouldn't litter," I said to Roofus on the way back to the trail. "I hope you're not a litterer. You know, besides the fertilizer you left back there."

Making our way further up the mountain, I found a garbage can and threw the wrapper away. Taking the last swig of my whiskey, I tossed the bottle into the trash can and said, "Hate to see a good thing end. But I guess all good things end. Right, Mom?" I looked up to the tops of the trees.

Roofus and I arrived at the summit as the sun was setting. Taking a load off on an old hand carved bench, I unlatched Roofus' leash to let him run around. As Roofus ran around in circles chasing his tail, I looked off into the sunset and admired the beauty that was quickly fading on the horizon.

What's the point of all this? I wondered as I watched Roofus.

Suddenly Roofus fell off an incline and out of sight. "Roofus!" I shouted, leaping out of my seat and scrambling to the edge. Looking over, I saw he had fallen into a ravine. It was steep, but I wasn't going to leave him there. "Hold on, buddy!" I shouted down at him. I stepped forward and began trying to make my way down the incline. Then suddenly, my foot hit something and I went tumbling down and everything went black.

CHAPTER 9

Blinking my eyes open, they adjusted to the bright light from atop the trees. My whole body hurt as I tried to move.

"Hey," Cole said, towering over me and blocking the sunshine.

I moved a hand up and shielded my eyes to get a better look at him. "Cole? What are you doing out here?" I asked as I began to sit up and lean against a log.

"I came looking for you after I talked to Emily. I was worried. And I had good reason! I found you lying in this ravine last night. I would have woken you, but you looked peaceful."

I scoffed. "Had about a fifth of whiskey, that's why I looked peaceful." I moved the blue blanket that Cole must have laid over me and looked around.

Cole shook his head as he sat down beside me. "For the record, I did try waking you up later into the night, but you wouldn't budge." Roofus walked over to Cole just then, and Cole patted his head. "Alcohol isn't the solution for the pain you have inside of you right now, Kane."

I laughed as I tried moving. "My body is killing me and I'm pretty sure a drink would ease that pain." I glanced over at the incline that I had tumbled down. "Dang... at least I can move. There's some pretty nasty looking rocks there I could have hit."

Cole looked up at the incline and nodded. "Yep. And you're lucky I found the dog leash sitting on the bench up there... I would have never looked over that ledge for you."

"It's a miracle," I said with a wry smile, looking over at Cole. I spotted a bandaid on the corner of his eyebrow and I recalled the altercation back at the firehouse. "Why'd you even come? After what happened at the station?"

Cole smiled over at me. "You can call me names, hate me or even punch me, but that won't change the bond we have. We're brothers for life." He reached over and grabbed his backpack I didn't notice and pulled out a water bottle. Handing it to me, he said, "Don't get me wrong. I don't like being punched... but I knew you were struggling and I wanted to come find you regardless."

I took a drink and wiped my mouth. "Thanks. How'd Emily even know where I was?" I asked.

"She said you came up here when Kyle passed. I guess you have a history of going off the grid kinda when these kind of things happen."

I laughed. "I kind of do... I just like to get alone with my thoughts. Try to figure it all out."

"Or avoid it," Cole replied. "Don't you dare try to punch me again," he said, holding up a hand to block me. We both laughed. "But honestly, drinking and running away from everything isn't really dealing with it, man. I mean that in the nicest way possible."

I nodded. "I know."

"Why not choose God? You do believe in Him," Cole said. "I'm not trying to offend you..." Cole paused and shook his head. "You know what? I am offending you and I don't care, man. You gotta buck up and pull yourself up by your bootstraps. Drinking and driving, Kane? Seriously? What needs to happen for you to wake up to God's truth?"

"Tell me how you really feel..." I replied, laughing slightly.

"Sorry. It's just confusing..." Cole said.

"It's alright." I knew Cole was concerned about me. He was here for me when nobody else had shown up. "Whiskey is something I can see. Something I can taste. Whiskey therapy can kick in pretty quick. A matter of minutes... ya know? It's just quick."

Cole nodded. "God's work does take more of a time investment, but its everlasting."

"Yeah..." I replied.

Cole put his hand on my shoulder and shook it lightly. "God loves you, Kane. And you do believe in Jesus."

"I do," I replied.

"You will see your mom again. In Heaven. You don't have to grieve like this world does. You grieve with hope. And really... a bottle isn't going to fix anything. It's not therapy. It's avoidance. Instead of that, you gotta dig deep into God and find that joy that only He can bring you."

"It's just easier to go for the bottle..."

"Yeah. But we both know easy doesn't translate into good, Especially when it comes to the heart," Cole replied.

My sister pushed against my mind just then. I knew our mother's passing would be traumatic and that she needed hope. "You know what?" I said.

"What?"

"Drinking isn't ever going to help my sister believe in God. And I want her to believe..."

"That's true..." Cole replied. "If you want her to end up at the foot of the cross, you gotta show her a reason why. Sure, you can talk about Heaven, but so can the unsaved people of this world. We have to be different. We have to be set apart from the world, Kane. And show that."

"I know..." I replied softly with my chin dipped to my chest.

"Don't be discouraged. Just repent and turn away from this life. Instead of trying to have one foot in the world and one foot in God, just go all-in with Him."

"I agree. I need to go all in. I don't feel any happier by drinking... but something like this talk... it energizes me."

"That's the power of God. He won't stop you from being sad, but He can give you hope. And He can give you joy."

"Thank you, Cole."

"You're welcome," he replied.

I took another drink of my water and rubbed behind the ears of Roofus. "We should get out of here," I said.

"Alright," Cole replied. Standing up, he asked, "Can you walk?" he asked.

I glanced down at my legs and saw one leg was bloodied and pretty banged up. "I didn't notice that... uh, I don't know." I set the water bottle down and began to pull myself up onto the log. Putting pressure on the messed up leg caused spikes of pain to shoot up through my ankle. "Ahh!" I shouted.

"Yeah... I don't know about that," Cole replied, looking down at my leg.

"I don't know either..." I replied. Cole came closer to me and I wrapped an arm around his neck for support. He helped me up out of the ravine and back down the trail to my car.

"Luckily, it's the left foot," I said as I opened my door and let Roofus jump in the back. "I'll still be able to drive."

Cole nodded. "That's good. What's your plan?"

"I'm going to go back to my mom's house and take care of this wound and relax."

"Stay off the bottle," Cole said, worried.

I smiled. "I will."

"Alright. I'm going to head back to Spokane. Let me know if you need anything."

"Oh, hey," I said.

Cole stopped and looked over at me from his truck. "Yeah?"

"So I guess Jensen canned me?"

Cole shook his head. "Nah... I got everyone to agree nothing ever happened and you left because of your mom."

"Really?" Remembering the phone call from the Chief, I asked, "But Jensen called last night."

"Probably to offer condolences. I'd call him back about bereavement."

"Ahh, that makes sense. I will give him a buzz. Thanks for everything, Cole."

"No problem." He smiled. "Take it easy, McCormick."

Getting into my car, I was overwhelmed with thankfulness. Cole was not only my comrade and captain down at fire station 9, he was my best friend. Watching in my rearview mirror as Cole pulled out onto Tod Road, I thanked God for him being in my life.

After I arrived back at my mother's house, I managed to get myself showered and my leg wounds cleaned up. They were all surface wounds. Luckily my ankle didn't seem to be broken, just sprained, and Roofus seemed to be fine too. As I limped out of the bathroom and into the living room, I saw my mother's Bible sitting on the coffee table. Thinking about what Cole said, I knew I needed to turn more to God.

Sitting down on the couch, I set my cell phone down on the coffee table. I still hadn't powered it back on since the previous night. I picked up my mom's Bible and let the pages fall open in my hands. Thumbing through the pages was like watching a slide show of colors. My mother had used a variety of colored markers to highlight passages through the Scriptures. Stopping at the book of Galatians, I began to read a portion highlighted in blue. Chapter five, verse sixteen.

16. So I say, walk by the Spirit, and you will not gratify the desires of the flesh. 17. For the flesh desires what is contrary to the Spirit, and the Spirit what is contrary to the flesh. They are in conflict with each other, so that you are not to do whatever you want.

Mulling the scripture over in my mind, I prayed for God's guidance in the reading.

Show me what your Word means. Reveal the wisdom in the words I have read. Amen.

Lifting my eyes from prayer, I looked back to the Bible. Reading the word 'flesh' on the page, I began to analyze my life. Going in reverse, I backed up to the bottle of whiskey, the driving, the skipping town to get away. It was all about me, and I immediately felt convicted and repented right there on my mother's couch. Tears fell from my eyes, distorting the blue highlighted scripture I had just read. Watching the blue drip down the page I realized my mother was right about faith. I could feel God's spirit inside of me stirring and I could feel it pushing its way into my soul. My heartache over the loss of my mother wasn't leaving, but a new found peace was calming the raging seas.

After an afternoon of praying and getting right with God, I decided to turn on my cell phone. I was ready for the aftermath that was sure to come after my mother's passing.

Immediately after powering on my phone and gaining reception, the notifications rolled in. Social media posts to me offering condolences, text messages, voicemails, tweets and even a couple emails. Everything came through at once. I smiled with tears in my eyes as I saw my friends and loved ones reach out to me. I looked up to God and thanked Him for His help through this and prayed I'd be able to use this time to witness to others.

Checking my voicemail, I listened to the Chief's message. Cole was exactly right, he was offering his condolences. He also told me to take as much time as I needed to grieve. The Chief recommended two weeks. He was a great guy. They all were at the station. It felt so good to have people that supported me like the brotherhood down at station 9. Sure, the distant relatives and friends online were nice too, but we didn't have a bond like I did with the guys at the station.

The voicemail was from Emily. She was wondering if I'd come help her break the news to Christopher. Right away, I sensed an opportunity for Christ to show through me in speaking with Christopher about his grandma passing. This will be good, I thought to myself. I stood up to head for the door to leave, but my ankle was still bothering me somewhat.

Roofus raised his head up from the love seat as I fell back to my prone position on the couch. Looking over at him, I said, "Don't judge me."

He lowered his head back down over his paws and closed his eyes.

Pulling up Emily's name in my contacts, I called her. It went straight to voicemail. Without leaving a message, I hung up. Glancing at the time, I saw it was already after four o'clock. Looking again over at Roofus with his eyes closed, I said, "That's a good idea." I adjusted my head into a more comfortable position on the couch and closed my eyes.

CHAPTER 10

Setting my burrito down I got from the hot case, I looked at the cashier behind the register.

"This going to be it?" the older gentleman asked.

I nodded.

"$4.67," he said, adjusting the toothpick between his teeth.

I looked at the burrito with a lowered eyebrow as I pulled my wallet out of my back pocket. Highway robbery, I thought to myself as I gave him my debit card. "That's a spendy burrito. Worth the money?"

He took my card and shook his head. "Nah... but it's the only place to get a bite for quite a while. So it's the best you can find."

I nodded. "Oh, joy." Taking my card back, I thanked him. Walking outside with my burrito, I spotted Kristen pumping gas at one of the pumps. I lowered my head and tried to hurry to my car parked alongside the gas station.

"Kane?" she asked before I could get around the corner of the building.

I took a deep breath and turned around. Forcing a smile, I said, surprised, "Kristen?"

"What are you doing up here?" she asked.

"Just grabbing some food before I head back to Spokane."

"I see... Do you know people up here?" she asked.

I nodded. And then shook my head. "Kind of... my mother."

"Kind of?"

"I... well... my mom. She just passed away..."

She gasped. "Oh my gosh, I'm so sorry..." She reached out and touched the side of my arm.

Confusion set into my mind by her soft and kind way about her and caused me to take a step back. "Why are you acting like you aren't mad at me now?"

She looked out towards the highway and dipped her chin as a breeze pushed her strands of blonde curls in the wind. "I was upset the other day. I was really into you and then I got blindsided by this crazy past of yours."

"You can't hold what I've done against me... that's not right. Besides you have a son, I am sure your past isn't perfect either!"

"I know..." she said, stepping closer to me. "I just don't want to get hurt again... I'm scared, Kane. I lost Blake's dad to him returning to the same type of past you have... But I know that's not fair to you."

I nodded. Looking at her car, I asked, "One person can't ruin life for us all, right?"

She nodded.

"Anyways... What are you doing up this direction?"

"I'm visiting my dad. He's the pastor over at the church in town."

"Cool. You just have a family full of churchgoers, eh?"

She laughed. "Yeah. Faith has been a pretty important part of my family."

"That's neat," I replied, smiling. My stomach made a grumble and I said, "I better get on the road and get this food in my belly."

She smiled. "Alright. See you around?"

I nodded. "Sure, I'd like that."

I couldn't keep the smile off my face after seeing Kristen, she had that effect on me. There was still a lot in the way of an 'us' but I was a little more hopeful now that we've settled that our pasts don't define us.

Roofus barked as I made my way to my car, jolting me out of my thoughts.

Opening my car door for him to jump in, I said, "Come on, Boy. Let's go see Ems."

Out of the Ashes

CHAPTER 11

Pulling up to Emily's house, I saw Christopher sitting on the porch with his eyes glued to his phone. Roofus stuck his head between the seats from the back and I asked him, "You want to see Emily and Christopher?" His tail began wagging and I smiled. "Okay. I gotta talk to Christopher with Emily first and then I will come get you. But first, you gotta lay down." He curled up on the back seat and lay prone. "Good boy!" Opening the car door, I saw Christopher look up at me for a moment.

"Hey, Uncle Kane," he said from the steps. I

kept my window down and left Roofus behind in the car. Emily and I wanted to ease Christopher into the reality of his grandma passing. Seeing Roofus would be an immediate giveaway to what had happened.

"How's it going?" I asked, coming around the front of my car. Looking up the sidewalk to my right, I saw Old Man Smiles coming our direction. He smiled and waved to me. I waved back.

"Good. Just trying to beat this level," Christopher replied, not looking up from his phone. I nodded and looked his direction as I continued up the path to the house.

"Cool," I replied.

"What's going on? What are you doing here?" Christopher asked, stopping his game and putting his phone in his pocket. He spotted my mother's bills in my hand.

I felt kind of stuck in the situation, but luckily Emily opened the front door just then. "Kane," she said with a relieved sigh. "Come on in. You too, Christopher."

As we walked inside, Christopher went down the hall headed for the restroom. "How'd you manage to keep it from him?" I asked.

Emily glanced down the hallway and waited

for the bathroom door to shut. Then, she looked back at me. In a whisper, she said, "I kept cooped up in my room, and said I was sick."

"Oh, I see." I sat down on the couch and Emily joined me. Handing her the bills and will, I said, "That should be it. There's her utilities and a few other bills. Not a whole lot."

Emily nodded. "Mother was pretty conservative."

"I never got the whole 'no T.V.' thing," I replied.

"It's of the devil!" Emily laughed with a mocking tone.

I grinned. "Don't mock her, Ems. You know there are some bad shows out there."

"Yeah, sure. But I think she just didn't want the extra expense."

I nodded in agreement.

Christopher came walking out from the hallway and looked over my shoulder through the living room window. "What's Roofus doing here?" he asked, his voice slightly worried.

"We need to talk," Emily said, standing up.

"Have a seat on the recliner," I said, nodding over to the chair.

"You guys are freaking me out… it's grandma, isn't it?" Christopher asked as he sat down.

Emily nodded and began crying into her hands as she sat back down on the couch. I placed a hand on her back to comfort her. Wiping her tears away, she looked up at Christopher. "I just want you to be okay, Christopher. I know how much she meant to you."

"I honestly didn't see her very often, Mom."

Emily tilted her head and shook it. "So? Why's that matter?"

He shrugged. "I just don't have a huge attachment to her. I know I got a little freaky the other day, but Kane and I talked it out the other day. She's going to Heaven."

Emily shook her head and narrowed her eyes over at me. "How dare you," she said as she stood up and stormed out of the room and down the hallway.

Going after her, I said, "Oh, come off it, Emily. There's no reason to withhold hope from a child!" She went into her bedroom and slammed the door.

"Why is she acting like a teenage girl?"

Christopher asked.

Looking back at him, I said, "Have a little compassion. Our mom just died." I took a deep breath in and let it out. "People process things differently and for your mom and her beliefs..."

Christopher interrupted me. "She doesn't believe in anything..."

"I know," I replied.

"So why would you say her beliefs?"

"If I wasn't interrupted, you would have heard it." I sat back down on the couch, close to the edge that was near the recliner Christopher was in. "Without a belief in Heaven... she grieves with no hope. It's different when someone dies and you don't believe in Heaven."

He nodded. "I was freaked out until you mentioned Heaven."

"Exactly," I replied with a nod.

Suddenly Emily's bedroom door cracked open and we both looked up as she came out of the hallway. My sister's eyes were red and swollen. She looked so sad, it tore me to pieces.

"I want to know about Heaven," she said as she came into the living room and sat on the edge of the recliner next to her son.

I smiled partially and nodded. "What do you think it is?"

She shrugged. "I don't know. Never spent a whole lot of time on the topic back in my church days... Floating spirits and angels? Harps and clouds?" She sighed. "I know it's stupid."

I shook my head. "No, it's a pretty common misconception."

"So then, tell me about it," she replied.

"I don't know a whole lot. But I know that God is going to create a new Heaven and a new Earth and it's going to be amazing. There won't be any pain, heartache or any sin whatsoever in Heaven. Our loved ones will be there that accepted Jesus Christ as their Savior and we'll spend eternity with God."

"Eternity is a long time... I'm so scared it'll be boring," Emily replied. "I don't want to go to a never ending church service."

I shook my head at her. "I don't think it's going to be like that, Ems."

"I like this life, Kane. I have passions and happiness with lots of things in this world."

"And why won't that be in Heaven? God created us in His image. He fashioned us to make art, to have passion and to enjoy all His creation has to offer. That's not going to change. What will change is the pain, the sin and the fallen state of man."

Emily began crying as she shook her head. "I don't know how to believe that."

I stood up and came over to her. Christopher reached up and rubbed her back. I crouched on my knees and looked at her as she had her chin dipped into her chest. "Ems. Mom told me the day before she died that you have to have faith, and faith is felt with the fingertips of your soul."

"What does that mean?" Emily asked.

"Well, your soul is who you are. Your mind, emotions and basic drive for life. When you decide to trust in God, you are investing yourself—your soul— into Him. When you make this decision, the one to trust God and believe in the death, burial and resurrection of Jesus Christ, you receive the Holy Spirit. Then, when that Spirit is allowed to flourish and is being fed, everything in your life begins to flourish based off that original faith and trust you placed in God."

Emily had a blank look on her face.

"Example: I powered on my phone after not having it on through the onslaught of people reaching out to me for condolences. When the notifications all came tumbling in at once, I would have been overwhelmed, but God's Holy Spirit was there to help me. His Spirit is working in all avenues of my life since I decided to walk in the Spirit instead of the flesh, with a fully committed life to Him. Everywhere I go, everywhere I look, I can find evidences of God working in my life."

She nodded. "Every time my phone would ding with a notification my heart would twist in pain."

"See? I didn't have that," I replied.

"But... what about the initial part of that? The initial faith?"

"That's believing in the death, burial and resurrection and placing your trust, aka faith, in Christ Jesus as your Lord and Savior."

She nodded slightly. "So, he makes you not sad about Mom?"

I shook my head. "I'm devastated by the loss of our mother. But I don't grieve like this world does. I grieve with hope. I know I'll see mom in Heaven down the line."

"There's plenty of people who don't believe in God who believe in Heaven," Emily retorted.

"Yeah. But they don't know if it's true. They just kind of cruise through life, hoping it'll end up the way they want. We on the other hand have the Scriptures and promises from God himself that give us a different kind of hope. A real hope. And God comforts us in our pain."

"I believe it all!" Christopher said, wiping tears from his cheeks.

Emily looked over at him. "Really?"

He nodded. "Kane experienced this, Mom. He's not reading it out of some church pamphlet or using a manuscript. He's talking about something that really happened to him!"

She looked back at me. "I want to believe so desperately... but logically, I can't. It's why I went to church for years but never made the commitment. It's just... not for me?"

I nodded as I knew she was on the right track. Given more time, my sister would be soon at the foot of the cross. In God's time, not mine. Looking at Christopher, I asked, "Do you want to accept Jesus into your heart as your Lord and Savior?"

He nodded.

I smiled. "Let's go over a few things and then we'll pray."

CHAPTER 12

After an eventful afternoon, I wanted to treat Christopher out to eat in celebration of his new found faith in Christ. Emily stayed in the kitchen and bedroom through most the afternoon while Christopher and I prayed and talked about his new life in Christ. I was a bit worried when I pitched Emily the idea of tagging along out to dinner with us, since she had been avoiding us since Christopher's commitment.

"Hey, Sis," I shouted from the couch in the living room.

"Yeah?" she replied, from the kitchen.

"Want to go grab some food with us? I am going to treat Christopher out to celebrate."

She turned the faucet off in the sink, and came to the doorway that connected the living room to the kitchen. "Seriously?" she asked.

"What?" I responded, confused.

"Mom's gone and you want to go have a celebratory dinner? You sure don't seem upset..." She returned to the dishes in the sink.

I followed after her. "Of course I'm upset about mom!" I said. "But your son just accepted Jesus into his heart and that's amazing and should be celebrated."

"I guess I just don't get it," she replied, shaking her head as she continued loading the dishwasher.

"I guess you don't..." I turned to leave the kitchen.

"Wait!" she said, grabbing onto my shoulder. "I'll go... I don't understand it... but I'll go. I'm happy for him."

I smiled. Hugging her, I said, "Thank you. I love you."

"I love you too," she replied.

"I'm hungry," Christopher said as he walked into the kitchen. "When are we going?"

"Let's go right now," Emily said, pushing out a half-smile. I knew she didn't get it, but I was happy she was trying, at least for Christopher.

As we sat down at a booth in the restaurant, I spotted Fred Foster over at a table with a few other officers in blue. "There's the guy who arrested me," I said, nodding towards his table as I scooted into the booth next to Emily.

She looked over and asked, "Which one?"

"The one with the short, curly brown hair."

She scoffed. "He looks like a tool."

I shook my head. "No, he's not. He does a lot of great work for this city. I think he misunderstands what happened at the Christmas party."

Emily raised her eyebrows over at me. "Wow... the way you've talked about him in the past, I thought you hated the guy."

"Yeah, me too. I just feel different towards

him now," I replied. Thinking about God, it made me realize it was due to Him. "It's a God thing."

Emily said nothing, but smiled.

Looking over at Christopher, I saw him squinting as he stared out the window. "What's on your mind?" I asked.

Looking to the both of us, he said, "Maybe if I can start going to that church, I can go to more LAN parties and stuff with Blake and the youth. Ya know?" Christopher's eyes were wide and excited. Suddenly the waitress came over to the table.

"What can I get you guys to drink?" the server asked as she passed out the menus.

"Cola," Emily and Christopher said.

"I'll take a water," I replied.

"I'll be right back, I need to go to the restroom," Christopher said as he slid out of the booth and headed to the bathroom.

"I'll get those drinks out," the server said, leaving the table.

"I don't think he's going to be able to go to youth group," Emily said.

I looked over at her. "How come?"

"I just don't see how that'll work... I'm gone a ton and he's not able to drive or anything."

"I'm sure someone will pick him up. He did manage to get a ride home from the LAN party with no effort on my part," I said as the server returned with our drinks. She placed each glass in front of us and dropped three straws in the middle of the table. "Thanks," I said to her and she left again.

Emily reached out and grabbed one of the straws. Putting it into her soda, she said, "I don't see a benefit in him going to church at all."

"C'mon, Ems. You know church helps. First hand..." I replied.

"Don't remind me of my past."

"Oh, you don't like that?" I laughed.

She smiled.

"Plus, he's running with a bad crowd.. That friend of his I saw the other day at your house. They were smoking pot."

She furrowed her eyebrows. "You don't know that," Emily said.

"Actually he's right," Christopher added as he sat back down in the booth.

"Really? You've been doing drugs?" Emily asked, looking up at him.

Christopher dipped his head to his chest as he scooted the rest of the way back into the seat. "I'm sorry, Mom."

Emily's eyes began watering. "I don't get it, Christopher. I try so hard to give you everything you want!"

He looked up at her with tears in his eyes. "But all I ever wanted was more time with you."

I could sense Emily's stress building up inside as she rubbed her shoulder. She had spent so many years working to become a surgeon and now her son was feeling neglected. I tried to ease the tension. "You have to make the right choices for yourself, Christopher. Your mom can't make them for you."

Emily looked over at me. "He's just a kid, Kane."

"True. But that doesn't mean he doesn't know what is right and wrong." I looked over at Christopher. "You knew smoking pot was wrong, didn't you? That's why you scrambled when I showed up and your buddy ran out the door?"

"Yeah..." Christopher replied. "But it doesn't

matter anymore."

"Why?" Emily asked.

"I don't even want to do it anymore, Mom. That's the cool thing about my new life in Christ," Christopher replied, glancing my direction. "Now that I have God... I don't feel like I need that stuff. I feel I have purpose and I was uniquely made in the image of God! The world is my oyster, Mom. Don't you get that? I can do all things through Christ which strengthens me. I feel so happy knowing that I'm a child of God." He beamed with pride in Jesus.

Emily let a laugh out and Christopher went red in embarrassment. I furrowed my eyebrows at her.

"I'm sorry," Emily said to both of us. "I didn't mean to laugh. I just... so don't get this God thing." She sighed.

"And you won't until you experience it. It's just something you have to go through to understand," I said.

I glanced over and saw Fred make eye contact with me from the table across the restaurant. He stood up and put his napkin down on his plate. He began to walk over to our table and I began to shift in my seat.

"Great... he's coming over," I said to Emily.

"Kane! I thought that was you!" Fred said dryly.

"Yep, sure is," I replied with a respectful nod.

He looked over at Emily and smiled. "Who's this hottie?"

Emily flashed a smile and grabbed for the dessert catalog on the table.

I jumped up from my seat and stood eye-to-eye with him. I felt an overwhelming desire to hit him in the moment. But I prayed quickly for self-control. Moving away from the table, I said, "That's my sister back there, man!"

He grinned. "Even better."

"I know what you are trying to do and it's not going to work," I replied.

He laughed. "Oh yeah? Tell me. How's the suspension going?"

"Look –I'm sorry about what happened at the Christmas party," I said.

He stopped smiling. "Why are you bringing that up, Kane?"

"I never said I'm sorry... and I truly am."

He scoffed. "You can start by apologizing for kissing my girlfriend."

"I didn't kiss her. She kissed me. That's the truth. But I want to apologize for every letting her get close to me."

"It's been a long time, Kane. You don't have to lie."

"I know I don't have to lie. And that's why you should believe me. I didn't kiss her."

He nodded as his lips perched to form a thin line. "Thank you. But I'm not changing my report."

I nodded. "I know you won't change it. That's not what I'm trying to get from this. I'm just saying sorry for the way it went down."

His vindictive self didn't have anything else to say. "Well, I'll see you around, Kane." He turned and went back to his table. Watching as he walked back over to his seat, I saw Old Man Smiles grabbing food from a plate someone left, on his way to the bathrooms.

"Is Old Man Smiles homeless?" I asked as I sat back down to the table with Emily and Christopher.

Christopher said, "Yes."

I waited for him to come back out of the restroom and I got up from the table again. "I'll be right back."

Walking across the restaurant, I came up to Old Man Smiles. "Sir?" I said.

He looked up at me and smiled. "Yes? I got lots of places to go and lots of people to see. So if you could step aside, it'd fill me with glee."

"Could I buy you some food?" I asked.

He paused and his smile fell away for a moment. "Why would you buy me food? Are you trying to convince yourself that you're good?"

"No. I just want to help."

"How about a twenty dollar bill instead? I'll eat elsewhere and a few of my friends can also be fed."

I laughed to myself as I pulled out my wallet and handed him a twenty. "Here."

"Thank you," he replied. His smile returned and he tipped his top hat as he continued on out of the restaurant.

Returning back to my booth, Christopher asked, "Why'd you give him money?"

"He needs it," I replied.

"You should have just bought him food if you wanted to help. You don't know what he'll do with the money," Emily said.

I nodded. "I offered him food, but he declined and wanted cash so he could help others. He's a funny guy, have you ever talked to him?"

"No... but you believed him?" Emily asked.

I shrugged. "It's not about what he does with the money, Ems. It's about doing what I could in the moment. I would have spent about the same on a meal here for him alone."

"How do you know he won't just go to the nearest liquor store?" Emily asked. "Rosy has seen that guy in there a ton."

"He might just go buy booze. I don't know? But that's not my worry. God will take care of the details. My responsibility is stepping out in faith." As the words rolled off my tongue with not even so much of a thought on my end, I knew it was of God and not me and I marveled in His awesomeness of Spirit and truth.

CHAPTER 13

A light drizzle fell on the morning of my mother's funeral three days later. I had been staying on Emily's couch. I wanted to be near the only family I had left until the funeral. Every ounce of me that morning didn't want to go to the services. I loved my mother dearly, and more than any other person on the face of the earth, but the thought of seeing her again, lying in a casket terrified me. A final goodbye to the woman that raised me wasn't at all what I wanted. I didn't want a final goodbye, I didn't want a goodbye at all. I knew it was what I had to do, no matter how uncomfortable it made me. And I knew God would help me.

"Kane..." Christopher said from behind me as I stared out Emily's living room window at the rain falling outside.

"Yeah?" I replied softly, but not turning to look at him. I didn't want him to see the tears that were running down my cheeks.

"Emily's freaking out in her bedroom again..." he replied.

Turning to him, I wiped the tears from my cheeks and looked him in the eyes. "She's 'mom' to you." I looked past him towards the hallway that led back to her room. "I'll go talk to her." Looking back at Christopher, I asked, "You okay?"

He nodded. "It's a little harder today... but I'll be okay."

I nodded at him and proceeded through the living room. Walking down the hallway, I could hear the sound of Emily's cries strengthen as I came closer to her door. Each step, my heart felt as if it was twisting inside my chest and reaching up to my throat, clenching it tightly.

I pushed open her bedroom door to find her on her knees in a mess. Her mascara was running, her hair was frazzled and pictures of mom were strewn all around her. "What's going on, Sis?"

She looked up at me with those sad and swollen eyes I had been seeing a lot of lately. Making eye contact with her, I felt a piercing pain shoot through me. It felt like a javelin tore through my torso. She sniffled and said, "She's really gone, Kane..."

I sat down on the floor next to her and brought my knees up to my chest. "I know..." I said, softly.

"I don't want to say goodbye," she said.

Dipping my head to my chest, I said, "Me either." Lifting my head back up, I put my arm around Emily. Her head rested against my shoulder, and I said, "We still have each other, Sis."

She looked up at me. "Tell me everything is going to be okay, Kane," she said.

"It's going to be okay."

"That didn't help," she replied as she began crying harder.

"I'm sorry, Sis."

"Can we pray?" she asked.

I nodded and we both bowed our heads.

I began praying, "God... Please help us to be able to get through today. Please help Emily as she tries to play a gracious host to the people at the funeral and the reception afterwards. Give her your strength. Give her your peace. Give her your comfort. In your name, we pray, Amen."

"Amen," she said.

I didn't really understand why Emily wanted to pray at that moment. She didn't have any belief in God, but I wasn't going to poke or prod at her about the reason, I just went along with it. There was no desire to disturb or disrupt any work that was going on inside of her in regards of her coming to Christ. Rising up to our feet, she looked at me and began to adjust my black tie. I wasn't able to control a slight laugh that escaped my lips in the moment.

"What?" she asked.

"Your adjusting my crooked tie while you have mascara running down your cheeks and your hair looks like Medusa's..."

She laughed and revealed that smile I so desperately longed to see on my sister's face again. I didn't want her to be in pain and it was comforting to see her smile even if it was only for a moment. "Yeah..." she said. "I need to get fixed up." She walked past me and headed into the bathroom to get ready.

Walking into the viewing room at the funeral home, my emotions were heightened. I was so scared as I approached my mother's coffin that I became light-headed and my feet felt like blocks of concrete. I didn't want to do it. But my sister was by my side and said, "C'mon, Kane." And as I heard it, my blocks of concrete loosened, and I felt okay again.

We walked up to the coffin and looked inside. There she was. She looked happy and peaceful.

"I'm going to miss her," I said as I felt tears well behind my eyes.

"Me too," Emily said, leaning her head onto my shoulder.

Looking back over towards the doorway, I saw Christopher stepping in and out as if he was debating on coming in. Shrugging Emily gently off my shoulder, I said softly, "I'm going to talk to

Christopher for a moment."

I went over to him and said, "You'll regret it if you don't say goodbye."

"Yeah," he said, looking past me towards the coffin. "It just feels really weird. This whole thing."

I nodded. "Kind of eerie, I know."

"Yeah, exactly," Christopher replied. "How'd she look?"

"She looked peaceful... It's really weird, but it's nice to get closure."

He nodded and looked past me again. "Okay, I'll go in." We walked back inside the viewing room and Emily came away from the coffin as Christopher went towards it.

"Thank you for talking to him," she said, stepping next to me.

"You're welcome," I replied. We watched as Christopher said something to his grandma at the coffin, then he began to cry. Emily left my side to comfort Christopher. Putting a hand on his shoulder, she began talking to him. She's a good mom, I thought to myself.

As they backed away from the coffin, I returned to it. Looking at my mother again, I said, "I love you, Mom. I'll do my best to watch over Emily and Christopher until I join you in Heaven." I retrieved a single white rose from the bouquet that sat on a table in the viewing room and placed it on her chest. We all three left the viewing room together and made our way down the hallway to where the funeral service was going to be held.

Sitting down in the front row, we all three remained quiet for a few moments. Then, Emily spoke. "I don't want to deal with all these people that are going to be showing up..."

"I'll help," I replied.

"Me too," Christopher added.

She smiled at both of us as she wiped her eyes.

Glancing around, I spotted Kristen towards the back of the room and I about freaked out. What was she doing here? Was she stalking me now?

"Excuse me," I said to Christopher and Emily as I stood up. Going back to her, I pulled her outside the room out of earshot of my sister and nephew.

"What are you doing here?" I asked.

"I'm filling in for one of my servers. Stix is catering the reception afterwards."

I rubbed my chin as I looked upwards to the ceiling.

"What?" she asked. "Am I that bad?"

Shaking my head, I said, "It's not that... It's just awkward. It's a very intimate time with my family."

"I'm sorry. I didn't know this was for your mom."

I nodded. "Okay. Can you get someone else to cover? I don't mean to be rude... It's just really weird to see you right now."

"I'm in management. I was already the last option. Trust me, they pulled me from my vacation because they were that shorthanded."

I took a deep breath in and said, "Okay. Let's not get crazy about this. Just... Try to keep your distance from us."

"Okay," she replied softly. She reached out and touched my arm, "I'm really sorry about your mom. I'm going to be busy in the kitchen the entire time, I promise you won't see me."

'Thanks," I said as I turned and headed back inside the room to Emily and Christopher. Returning back to my seat, they both had their eyes glued to me.

"Was that Kristen? What was she doing here? Is she leaving?" Emily asked, glancing towards the back.

"No. She's going to stay and cater."

"She works for Stix?" Emily asked, surprised.

"Yeah," I replied. "She's filling in for someone... She wouldn't be here if she didn't need to be."

Emily nodded. "Okay. You know what, Kane? I see that look in your eye about her. I wasn't going to tell you this because you don't like me to pry, but I feel it's for the best. That day she dropped off Christopher from the LAN party..."

"Yeah...?" I asked, leaning in.

"She showed up with some other guy and the guy's kid. That's why I told her all that stuff about you... I was just trying to protect you."

I had totally spaced the fact nobody explained to me how Kristen ended up talking to my sister. After feeling stupid, my lips perched as I felt anger begin to rise in me. I knew it was most likely Tyson, and that probably meant Kristen was lying about something not being there between them. Praying quickly without even closing my eyes, I asked God for His help. The next moment I felt the need to refocus back on the fact we were at our mothers funeral. I said, "Let's focus on today, Ems."

"It's just super awkward having her be here... but I guess that's my fault picking this place and not knowing she worked with Stix. I sure hope everything goes okay," Emily replied with a sigh.

"Ems. It will be okay, the place is still great. This won't be a problem."

After the funeral services, reception and the burial right outside the funeral home in the cemetery; it was time for the reading of the will and last testament. A lawyer notified Emily and I of the reading being held in a private room right in the funeral home.

Christopher wasn't allowed in the room since he wasn't mentioned in the will. My mother was old-fashioned like that. She figured Emily would take care of him and hand down any family heirlooms she felt he should have. As we sat down at the large executive table inside the room, the lawyer at the end of the table cleared his throat. "That was a beautiful service. Your mother would have been impressed," he said in a soft and genuine tone as he shuffled papers.

"Thank you," Emily said, smiling. I knew it meant a lot to Emily to hear that. She had spent a great deal of her safety net in the bank to pay for the services and arrangements. She was going to get it back with the life insurance policy, but it still took a lot of time which she wasn't going to get back.

We sat in silence for a minute before it became rather awkward. "Are you going to start the reading?" I asked, leaning out onto the table with my hands out.

"There's a missing party," he replied, glancing at his watch. "I told them the reading was at four o'clock, so we'll give him until five minutes past four."

"Who?" I asked, glancing over at the copy of the will that I retrieved from my mother's house that sat in front of Emily. "Emily and I were the only ones mentioned," I said, re-reading the will in my head.

The door opened and a man walked in. He was slender and had a half-beard that was neatly trimmed. His hair was dark and slicked back and he was wearing a black suit. He didn't make eye contact with Emily or me, but went directly up to the lawyer. "Mr. Johnson," he said, shaking the lawyer's hand.

"Who is this?" I asked, leaning across the table with my arm extended out towards the mysterious man. "He's not in the will at all."

"I've never seen this man in my life," Emily added, shaking her head.

"This is Timothy Raton," the lawyer replied. "He, in fact, is in the will."

Standing up, I headed over to the lawyer and showed him the will I had brought. "No, he's not!"

"Yes, he is!" Mr. Johnson retorted back pointing to Timothy's name in the will he had. "This is your mother's first child. She had him long before Kyle."

"What?" I asked, confused. Shaking my head, I said, "No... she didn't."

"She kept it from you."

"But our will doesn't have anything mentioning him."

The lawyer took the paper and looked at it. "Oh, I see."

"That's right!" I said with a confident nod.

"No... You're misunderstanding. What I meant was I now see what the problem is. The will I have is newer than yours."

"What?" I asked, leaning over the lawyer's shoulder. He pointed to the date on his copy and it was dated eight months after mine. "Why'd she change it?"

"What's the date?" Emily asked from across the table.

"August of last year," I replied. Then I realized it was after my mother's diagnosis of cancer.

Timothy chimed in. "I know you don't know me... but she contacted me before and after she found out about the cancer. I had been searching for our mother for years before the first time she reached out to me."

"Don't call her your mother," I warned.

"She's my mom too!" he retorted. "I was just given up! It doesn't make me lesser!"

"No... this doesn't make any sense," I replied, throwing my hands up. "She didn't have another kid!"

"She did," Timothy replied softly.

I left the lawyer's side and darted out of the room through the large doors. There was no way my mother did this to Emily and I. It was a setup. The way that lawyer and him shook hands. They were in on it together! I swear it!

"Kane?" Christopher said from the bench that sat up against the wall of the room. I was jolted from my thoughts. "Who was that guy that went in there?" Christopher asked upon approaching me.

Shaking my head as I looked at him, I said, "I don't know."

I left Christopher there outside the room and headed out the front doors of the funeral home. A breath of fresh air to clear my head and think for a moment was just what I needed. Sitting down on the funeral home's front steps, I bowed my head and prayed.

Dear God... Is this true? Did my mom really have another son that Emily and I never knew about? Please help me understand. Amen.

Lifting my head back up, I saw Kristen walking out a side door to the Stix van with a bunch of food trays in her arms. I got up and ran over to help. Grabbing a few of the large metal trays from the top of the stack, I smiled at her.

"Thanks," she said.

"You're welcome," I replied. Walking with her to the van, I opened the back doors and placed the trays inside.

"What are you doing out here?" she asked.

"I just needed to get out of there and clear my head..." I said. "Thanks for today by the way. I barely saw you."

She nodded. "No problem. I never intended to make things uncomfortable. I would have got someone over here to cover the catering gig if I could have."

I nodded. "Thanks. This might seem like an inappropriate time to ask, but I want to know something, Kristen."

"Sure, what is it?"

"Why were you with Tyson when he dropped off Christopher at my house?"

She sighed as she shifted her gaze to the ground. "I was just going to give Christopher a ride home, because Jacob's dad bailed and I volunteered... I wanted to see you, Kane... but I got a flat tire on the way and I called him. I just needed a ride."

"Hmm..." I replied.

She reached out and touched my arm. "There's nothing there between us. I promise."

"Okay-" I started to say.

"Kane, he's taking it all!" Emily shouted as she ran out of the funeral home and down the steps my direction.

"What are you talking about?" I asked, turning to her.

"He's taking all the money. I guess according to this new will, we get nothing!"

I looked over to the front doors of the funeral home to see Timothy walk down the steps with the lawyer. "We'll fight this in court," I replied.

"We don't have any money to fight it, I broke my bank just doing the funeral."

"I don't care what it takes. I'll sell my car if I have to." I glanced over to see Kristen going back in through the side door of the funeral home. I turned back to Emily. "He's not going to get away with this."

CHAPTER 14

The next day in my apartment, I waited for a phone call back from a lawyer's office I found in the yellow pages. The scam my mother's lawyer and this Timothy guy were trying to pull wasn't going to work with me. I was more than willing to sell my car to fund the cost of a lawyer to contest the will.

Suddenly a knock came from the door, breaking through my thoughts. Glancing at my phone, I saw it was only seven o'clock in the morning. Who could that be? I wasn't expecting anyone over, I thought to myself as I got up to go answer the door.

Looking through the peephole, I saw it was Cole. I opened the door and smiled at him with a confused look as I tilted my head. "Taylor?" I said, perplexed.

"I know it's weird I'm here... but we need to talk." I spotted an envelope in his hand.

"Why? What's up?" I asked.

"Are you going to invite me in?" he asked.

"Of course... sorry," I replied, letting go of the door letting it swing open. He came inside and shut it behind him.

"The football game went good the other day at the church if you were wondering," he said as he took a seat on the couch.

"Is that why you came over here so early?" I asked. Feeling a sense of rudeness in my tone, I quickly apologized. "Sorry. Just trying to deal with some personal stuff right now."

"About your brother?"

My jaw clenched. "He's not my brother... but how did you hear about that?" I asked, taking a seat on the couch next to him.

"Kristen. I saw her at the grocery store."

I sighed. "That wasn't her business to share... I didn't even tell her, she must have overheard my sister and I."

"She was just worried about you, but that's irrelevant, Kane." Cole picked up the envelope next to him on the couch and handed it over to me.

"What is this?" I asked, looking up at him.

"Open it."

Opening up the large unmarked envelope, I pulled out a vital record sheet. I was speechless. Timothy Raton was indeed my brother. My phone began ringing on the kitchen table. I ignored it knowing it was the lawyer calling me back.

"Aren't you going to answer your phone?" Cole asked, glancing towards the kitchen.

"It's a lawyer's office... I called to figure out how to fight this guy in court. But it looks like he's not lying about being my brother."

Cole nodded. "Nope, he's not lying." Cole leaned back and sighed heavily.

"How'd you get this?" I asked.

"Alderman's sister works in Vital Records in

downtown Spokane. Last night after Megan and I ran into Kristen at the grocery store, I wanted to see if it was true for myself so... I called him up."

Nodding as I processed the information, another knock came from the door. Glancing over at Cole, he shrugged at me indicating he didn't know who it was. Standing up, I set the envelope and papers down on the coffee table and went to answer the door.

"McCormick," Brian said as I opened the door.

"Hey, buddy. How are you?" I asked.

"Hey... I was on my way to work and wanted to let you know I was sorry about not being able to make the funeral yesterday." He looked past me at Cole on the couch. "Hey, Taylor."

Cole nodded to him. "Gomer."

I smiled. "No problem about not being able to come by the funeral. Someone's gotta fight those fires. Right?"

He nodded and then shrugged. "Didn't actually have any fires... but yeah. Someone's gotta be there just in case." Looking past me again, he said, "You coming in today, Taylor?"

Cole stood up and came over to the door.

"Yeah. I planned on heading to the station within the next few minutes."

Brian turned back to me and asked, "You holding up, okay? We miss you down at the station."

"Yeah. I'm okay. I'm missing work… but it's good to get family time in and whatnot."

"Well, hope to see you soon."

"You will," I replied, smiling.

Brian left and headed down the apartment stairs.

"I better get going to the station too," Cole said.

"Yeah. What's a shift without its Captain?" I said nudging him with my shoulder.

Cole grinned. He began leaving, but stopped and turned to me. "Hey, I heard you apologized to Foster."

"Sure did. And not just because you told me I should… I really believe God softened my heart when I saw him at a restaurant. I wanted to make things right with the guy."

"Well, it worked. He adjusted his report enough to let you off the hook. I think he knew you were just protecting Gomer. He was just mad." Cole patted my shoulder. "That was big of you to apologize to him."

"Thanks."

"I know you don't usually like to say you're sorry about these kind of things. Pretty mature, McCormick," He said smiling, as if he were talking to a child.

"Okay," I replied, laughing. "Enough!" I said, raising my hands.

He laughed. Glancing behind me at the coffee table where the vital record papers were, Cole asked, "Are you still going to contest the will?"

"I don't know if I can..." I replied.

"You can. When my father passed away, my brother was upset about not getting his inheritance. He contested it and won a pretty good chunk of the estate. My dad had cut him out because he wasn't happy with his sinful lifestyle."

"Really?" I replied.

"Yep. Technically, you have every right. I would do it. She cut you both out, something doesn't seem right," Cole said.

"Yeah," I replied. "But what if there is more

to the story? My mom wasn't ever careless with her decisions."

"How are you going to figure that out?" Cole asked.

"I think I'm going to go see him." I went over to the kitchen table and grabbed my phone and the new will that had Timothy's address on it. I also grabbed the vital record papers off the coffee table and shoved it into the envelope and headed out the door.

As I began to lock my apartment door, Cole asked, "You sure you're ready for this kind of thing? You don't know what kind of guy you are dealing with."

I locked the door and turned to him. I put my shades down over my eyes. "I can handle it."

"What about Emily?" Cole said.

"I'm going to go talk to her right now."

At Emily's, I turned off my car and hurried up to her front door. The door was unlocked, so I let myself in.

"Emily?" I hollered walking inside.

"Kane?" she said, coming out of her bedroom and down the hallway. Her eyes were swollen.

Coming up to her, I put my hands on her arms. "You alright? What's wrong?" I asked.

She shook her head and looked down. "I'm just upset about mom..."

"Why didn't you call me?" I asked.

She shrugged as she dropped her eyes onto my chest. "I didn't feel like I could be sad anymore.... The funeral was over and..."

"It's okay," I interrupted her, putting my arms around her. She must have spotted the envelope in my hand as she released from my hold quickly after I began to hug her.

"What's that?" she asked.

"Here," I said, handing it to her.

We sat down on the couch. As she pulled out the papers, I reached down and petted Roofus as he lay next to my feet. She dropped the paper into her lap and said, "Now what? We can't contest it?"

I said, "We can... but he's our brother."

She laughed. "Hardly. Sure, maybe because mom got knocked up as a teenager. But that makes him a brother by DNA, only."

I was confused by the harshness she was showing. "Aren't you a little surprised to have a brother? It's even from our dad!"

"No. I'm a little mad at her, actually." Emily shook her head. "Do you know how many lectures she gave me about how boys were bad? How many times she scolded me because of my boyfriends? She treated me like trash during some of my teenage years."

I sat back. "I think it was probably because she knew how it felt to give up a child... don't you?"

Emily sighed. "Maybe. But regardless, I'm contesting the will. I already phoned my lawyer last night and left a voicemail."

"On your own? How? I thought you were broke?"

"I'll take out a second mortgage on this house to get what's mine, if I have to!"

"Ems..." I said, softly.

"What? Seriously? Maybe it's because you didn't actually spend any money on mom's funeral, but I spent a ton."

"How much?" I asked.

She shook her head. "I don't even want to say it."

"How much, Ems?"

"$10,000..." she said.

"Wow."

"Yeah. I need to recoup that cost. I make good money, but my student loans are killing me." She paused for a moment before becoming more distraught. "Which I could have paid off with that money! He's a snake for coming in like this and swooping it all up from under us!"

"You're not money hungry, Emily," I said, sternly.

"I know... but she was our mom. He can't do this." She stopped and looked at me. "What's your plan? Just let him keep it all?"

"No. I'm going to go see him."

"What? Where is he?" she asked.

"He's in the Tri-Cities. The will the lawyer provided us had his address on it."

"And you're going to drive two hours away to meet this guy?"

"Yeah, I want to see what he's all about.

Mom was a smart lady. There's got to be more to this we are missing."

"Yeah. I thought she was smart until all this happened."

Shaking my head, I said, "Ems... Don't let this change your mind about who mom was. She was still a good person."

She laughed. "Okay. Good luck with your adventure. I'm still going to contest it."

I stood up from the couch. "I'll let you know what I find out." Looking around, I asked, "Where's Christopher?"

She smiled and said, "He's at another LAN party."

I grinned. "You let him go?"

She nodded. "I'm off work right now and all the parents are more than willing to help with rides once I go back. I think you were right about it being good for him."

I nodded. "He's at a crucial age right now... Hanging with the wrong group can mess him up for life."

"I know. He found out that Kegan kid he was hanging out with a while back got busted for driving without a license and possession. That happened on the same night you picked him up."

I felt chills run through my body. "See... That's a God thing right there."

She nodded. "Quite a coincidence to say the least."

Heading for the front door, I said, "I love you. Think about waiting on contesting the will. I'll keep you updated."

She smiled. "I love you too. I'll think about it."

CHAPTER 15

Stopping back at my apartment, I packed an overnight bag for my trip and a few extra sets of clothes. I didn't know how long I'd be down there, but I knew I didn't want to be forced to come back too quickly.

As I pulled up to the exit of my apartment complex, I saw a truck coming down the road too quickly. I stopped and waited for him to pass. While I was waiting, my phone rang. I looked over and reached for it. I wondered, who could that be...

Smash!

The truck smashed into the front driver side of my car, sending my car spinning into the street. The little island girl I had sitting up on the dashboard went flying in slow motion across my line of sight as I tried to yank on the steering wheel in some attempt to gain control. My head slammed against the window and my car came to a sudden stop.

My car horn was blaring as I reached up and felt blood running down the side of my temple. I opened my car door and stumbled out into the road.

Dear God, please let the other driver be okay. Amen.

Scrambling across the road, I made my way over to the truck. Leaning on the truck for support, I came around the back as I stumbled and grabbed onto my side that was hurting. Coming to the driver's door, I began reaching for the door handle and tumbled over in pain to the pavement. People came out from neighboring complexes to see what all the commotion was about.

"Sir!" a woman shouted as she approached.

Looking at her, I pointed to the truck behind me and said, "Make sure he's okay!"

"But you're bleeding!" she shouted.

"Don't worry about me!" I retorted as I felt a pain rip through my torso. Folding into myself, I fell over onto my side against the pavement. Another pain ripped through my side and I grabbed at it. Looking down, I saw more blood seeping through my clothing. "Ugh..." I cried out in pain.

Suddenly, Kristen dropped down into my view. "Kane?" she asked. "Can you hear me?"

I nodded quickly as I winced in pain. Sirens rang in the background as the pain grew more intense and then, darkness.

Coming alert in a hospital bed, I sat up. Looking over, I saw Kristen asleep in a chair. Dangling my feet over the side of my bed, I began ripping off the cords attached to me. An alarm sounded on one of the machines, startling Kristen awake.

"Sorry," I said as I removed the I.V. from my arm and stood up.

"What on earth are you doing?" she asked, as

she leaped up from the chair.

"I'm leaving," I replied as I headed over to the closet and opened the door. "I don't have time for this."

"What do you mean, Kane? You were in an accident and had glass lodged into your side. You need to heal up."

There was nothing in the closet. Turning to her, I asked, "Why were you even at the wreck?"

"I was driving by on the way home from the store and noticed your car."

"Okay. Where are my clothes?"

"They were all bloodied and trashed. They threw them away. I got this bag from your car though." She went over to the chair and grabbed the duffle bag. "I don't think you can leave the hospital, though, Kane..."

Grabbing the duffle bag from her hand, I unzipped it and said, "Watch me." I took the bag into the bathroom to change. As I was changing, I could feel pain shooting through my side. "Ahhh," I moaned.

Kristen was on the other side of the bathroom door. "Yeah... that's why you aren't supposed to leave yet..."

I laughed. "Am I going to die if I leave?"

"I don't think so. But I don't think they want you-"

Someone came into the room. Freezing in place, I stood up as I had one leg into my pair of jeans. "Where's Mr. McCormick at? It's time for his round of pain killers."

"I don't need those," I said loudly through the door as I continued getting dressed.

The woman knocked on the door and said, "You aren't thinking about leaving, are you?"

I laughed. "No, I'm not *thinking* about it." I finished getting my clothing on just then and opened the door. Looking at the nurse, I said, "I *am* leaving."

"Mr. McCormick. We need to monitor you for..."

I left the room with the duffle bag over my shoulder with no shoes on, not waiting for her to finish her sentence. I had my eyes on the exit down the hallway. Another nurse came up to me when I passed the nurse's station.

"You can go, but we need you to sign this release form," she said with annoyance. Walking with her over to the nurse's station, I signed my name on the paper and dropped the pen on the counter.

I turned and continued down the hall to leave. Kristen caught up to my side. "Are you crazy?" she asked, keeping my pace.

I looked over at her and said, "Maybe... Do you have my sunglasses?"

She shook her head and sighed as we came outside. It was already dark. "I don't think you'll need them..." she said.

"Well, the sun will come up tomorrow." I laughed.

"I didn't see them anywhere..." she replied, not amused.

"Okay. Where'd you put my car?" I asked, looking around the parking lot of the hospital. "Or whoever brought it up here. Oh wait... it's probably impounded or something." She was remaining silent, so I looked over at her.

She frowned.

"No..." I said, fearing the worst.

She shrugged. "Sorry, Kane. It's totaled."

I threw the duffle bag across the sidewalk in

frustration. "There's no way! I saw the damage! It wasn't *that* bad!"

She shook her head. "They said it was probably totaled."

"Who?" I asked, approaching her.

"The tow company, Edmunds? I asked them about it..." Knowing the owner and all the guys who worked at Edmunds, I knew their word was reliable.

Stopping, I realized I hadn't even thanked her for all she had done. She came with me to the hospital, grabbed my duffle bag and even asked the tow company about my ride. "Hey... Thanks for doing all you did for me. That was awfully nice of you..."

She nodded with her lips perched together.

"Okay, no car," I said quickly with a definitive tone. Looking around the parking lot and back towards the hospital, I said, "One question left on my mind... I don't know where my sister is... or the guys from the fire station. You would think they would show up..."

"I wasn't sure how you wanted it all handled... I didn't call anyone."

I nodded. "I'm actually glad you didn't call anyone. They would have freaked out and stopped me from leaving. But I guess you're trying to stop me too."

"I was a little concerned, but I didn't stop you."

"True," I replied. Looking down the sidewalk, I began heading for my duffle bag on the ground.

Kristen followed behind me. "So, where were you going?"

I glanced over my shoulder at her. "Why do you think I was going somewhere?"

"The overnight bag. And you made it pretty clear you wanted out of the hospital in a hurry..."

I picked up the duffle bag and turned around to her. "I was going to see my brother in the Tri-Cities."

Her eyes widened. "So, he *is* your brother?"

"Yep... But I don't have a car now..."

"Why don't I take you?" she asked.

I tilted my head a little. "Really? Don't you have work?"

"I'm still on vacation and Blake's out of town with his grandparents—the father's parents, in Moses Lake."

I thought about it for a second and then shrugged. It could be an opportunity to learn a little more about her, and I had to go see this guy regardless. "Why not? Let's do it," I said.

She smiled. "Alright. My car is this way."

Arriving in the Tri-Cities, we found a hotel in Kennewick, it was fairly close in proximity of the address we had for my brother. After getting checked in, we made our ways to our separate rooms.

Sitting down on my hotel room's bed, I pulled off my shirt and inspected my wounds. A couple good gashes in the chest and rib cage, but the worst was on the side. The side wound had a large bandage over it. Pulling it back, I glanced at the stitches. "Got me pretty good," I said out loud to myself, covering the wound back up. Lying down on my bed, I scooted myself up to the pillow and rested my head on it.

Looking out the hotel room window, I saw the moon was full and beautiful. I thought of my mother and how she was not a resident of earth anymore, but at home in Heaven with Kyle. There was no way I was ever going to understand what went through her mind and the reasons to why she gave up Timothy when she was younger, but at least I still had the chance to meet him. Even though my car was totaled and the money of the will would have helped me more than ever, I still felt the desire to know more. I didn't want to fight him for the money without knowing him. There had to be some reason why my mother would leave everything to him, and I needed to figure that out.

Closing my eyes, I began to pray.

Thank you Lord for saving my life today. If it wasn't for your protection, I could have died. I know my mom is doing better up there and tell her and Kyle I said 'hi.'

I opened my eyes as I heard a sound come from the next room over where Kristen was. I smiled and closed my eyes again.

Thank you for having Kristen come with me on this journey. I don't know what you want between us. But I hope your will be done in all matters. Help soften my sister's heart and allow your love to break into her world. Help her find you Lord. Thank you for Christopher finding You and help him enjoy the company of fellow believers. I love you Jesus, Amen.

Adjusting in my bed, I got under the covers

and reached to turn off the light on the night stand. As I reached for the light another surge of pain rushed through my side. The pain I was experiencing all over my body wasn't comfortable, but it was tolerable. And regardless of it, I had a lot to be thankful for.

CHAPTER 16

After a restless night of sleep, I woke up before the sun rose and went on the hunt for coffee. Walking into the hotel office, I spotted a coffee pot and cups. Looking over at the lady behind the counter, I smiled and said, "Good morning."

"Good morning," she replied, smiling back at me.

I walked over and poured a cup. Taking a sip, I almost gagged by the taste of it. Glancing around the pot, I saw the bag with the coffee grounds they used. Arabic Blend, gross, I thought to myself. Turning around, I tossed the cup into the garbage and left the office.

Getting onto the sidewalk outside the hotel grounds, I spotted a Starbucks up the road. Making my way there, I fought through the pain that gnawed at my side. I needed coffee more than I needed comfort. Walking inside the Starbucks, I was happy to see there was no line.

"I'll take a Triple Venti White Chocolate Mocha Brava with no whipped cream."

"Anything else?" the man asked as he penned notes on the cup.

I thought about Kristen. What would she want? I wondered. I went with my gut.

"Sir?" the man behind the counter said.

"Just make it two of those Ventis, please."

"Okay."

Getting back to the hotel, I saw Kristen standing in front of my hotel door, knocking. I smiled as I approached her. She began tapping her foot and looking back and forth down each way. I felt kind of bad as I laughed quietly. She was probably worried I died or something.

"Who are you?!" I shouted in a deep voice from right behind her, startling her. She jumped up and screamed as she twirled around. She laughed and smacked me in the shoulder.

"You freaked me out so bad!" she said, laughing.

I handed her a coffee and said, "I couldn't help it when I saw you." I smiled.

"Brat," she said, trying to hide her smile. She took a sip of the coffee and her eyes widened. "Wow... this is good," she looked at the cup and asked, "What is this?"

"Sweet nectar of the god's, of course," I replied.

She laughed. "Whatever it is, its yummy..."

I smiled. "Triple Venti White Chocolate Mocha Brava is the official title of it."

"That's a mouthful! It's delicious. I'll have to remember this for next time I get coffee."

"It's what I get every time."

"I usually just get Frappuccinos. I never know what to order and they have a million things on the menu board."

I laughed. "Yeah, that menu is ridiculous. I just get what my mom used to order."

She smiled. "That's cute."

Opening my door, I held it open for her to come inside. "Were you worried when I wasn't answering?" I asked as I followed her in and shut the door behind me.

She nodded. "I was standing there for like a solid ten minutes knocking... I wasn't sure if you were just a hard sleeper or if your wounds got the best of you."

"I couldn't sleep very well, so I got up early and went looking for coffee."

"Yeah? They had some in the office, I saw it last night."

I cringed. "I tried that stuff this morning... it was nasty."

She laughed and took another drink. "How are your wounds doing?"

I finished my coffee and tossed it into the garbage can. "They're okay." I got up and went over to my duffle bag. Pulling out the will, I said, "Thanks for grabbing this by the way."

"No problem... I grabbed whatever I could

find that looked important. Your cell phone is in there too."

"Cool," I replied. Looking at the address for Timothy, I pulled my phone out of the bag and programmed it in. After the directions loaded, I looked at Kristen and said, "Looks like it's only about ten minutes from here."

"We knew it was close, but that's super close! Let's go," she replied.

I nodded and smiled.

Getting into her car, I set the phone down in my lap and tried pulling on the seat belt, but that sharp pain in my side screamed out. "Ahhh!" I said.

"Need some help?" she asked.

"That'd be great," I replied, with a half-smile. I hated needing help, but appreciated her willingness.

Reaching over the armrest between us, she grabbed onto the seatbelt and began pulling it across my chest. A whiff of her hair blew into my face and I couldn't help but smile as she latched me in. She caught me smiling.

"What?" she asked.

I turned red in embarrassment. "Nothing."

"No... tell me why you were smiling like that, Kane."

"Okay... well, your hair," I paused and looked at her as her eyes were wide and fixated on me.

"Yeah? What about my hair?"

"It smells really good. I know that's weird... but I just like the way it smells." I shot one hand up in confusion of the words coming out of my mouth.

She laughed. "That's so funny you say that. I love the smell of my hair too. I have this special leave-in treatment I put in it."

"Really? They make stuff you leave in your hair?" I asked.

She smiled and replied, "Yeah, dork." She put her hand behind my seat and began backing out of the parking space.

Coming to a stop alongside the curb in a residential neighborhood, I double checked the address to make sure it was right. 5464 Sydney Ave. "That's it," I said, looking down at the will and then back up at the house. Looking over at Kristen, I saw her beaming. "What?"

"I'm just excited for you... this could be a start of a relationship with your long lost brother."

"My brother died in Iraq." I nodded the direction of the house as I continued, "This guy is just a DNA brother. Big difference."

She nodded as the smile fell away. Touching my arm, she said, "Well, regardless... I think it's brave to have a desire to come down here and meet him."

"Thanks," I replied, opening the car door. Closing it, I glanced at Kristen to see her waving from inside the car. I laughed and waved back at her.

Turning around, I looked the house over. It was red bricked, one level and had a cracking cement ramp leading up to the front door. Walking up the driveway, I came to the door. Giving it a firm knock, I stepped back and waited for someone to answer.

The door opened and an old man coughed as he pushed open the screen door. "Yes?" he said in a raspy voice.

"Hi. I'm looking for Timothy?"

He coughed again and spat on the porch, right next to an old worn rug. "You must be talking about Tim. He's not here right now. He's down the block at Dwayne's house."

I looked to the sidewalk and glanced around. Looking back at the old man, I asked, "Where is that?"

The gentleman stepped out from the screen door and pointed down the road. "Just go down to the pink house and turn right. But if you make it to the blue house, you went too far. Once you turn right at the pink house go to the white house and it's right next to that. It's a blue house."

"Okay..." I replied, laughing to myself at his extensive directions. "Thank you."

He shooed his hand out and said, "Don't worry about it." He began coughing again. "And if you do see him, let him know that the pharmacy called and the other half of Kyle's script is ready for pick up."

"Script?" I asked.

"Prescription." The old man squinted and asked, "You kind of slow or something?"

I shook my head. "No, Sir. Thank you."

He nodded and went back into the house

and shut the door. Walking down the driveway back to the car, I wondered to myself who Kyle was and what prescription he had. Did Timothy know my older brother Kyle when he was alive? Did he name his kid after him or something?

Coming back to the car, I got inside and shut the door.

"So?" Kristen asked.

I looked over at her and said, "He wasn't there, but he's at some guy's house named Dwayne?"

"Okay," she replied. "How do I get there?"

I laughed as I recalled the directions. "Turn around and go up and take your next right."

"Alright." Kristen pulled a u-turn and headed to the corner. "Who was that guy you were talking to?"

I shrugged. "Old... other than that, I don't know."

We turned onto the street and I pointed out the blue house. "There. That's where he said Timothy was..."

Getting out, I leaned back in through the car door and asked, "Want to go with me?"

She shrugged. "Sure." Getting out of the car, she looked over at the white house we passed. "That's a nice house. I like those pillars out front."

I glanced over. "Yeah, they're nice," I replied, admiring the look on her face as she looked at them.

Walking up the path to the house, we saw a few guys out in the garage that was attached to the house. Leaning to one side, I spotted him. My heart jumped a little seeing him again. This time I wasn't angry, I was more eager to meet him than anything else.

Veering off the path, Kristen and I headed up the driveway to the garage. Timothy came out with a beer in his hand and took a swig as we walked up. His ripped up jeans and flannel red cutoff shirt was a far cry from the suit I saw him in at the will reading.

He narrowed his eyes at me and ran his fingers through his greasy black hair. "What are you doing here?" he asked, tipping his chin. His friends came out of the garage and joined his sides.

"I just wanted to come meet you," I said.

He held out his arms and said, "Here I am."

Making eye contact with him and then the other guys, I asked, "Could we talk?"

He furrowed his eyebrows. "That money is

mine."

My eagerness to meet him was overwhelmed by anger as I felt every fiber of my being wanting to leap across the cement that separated us and beat him to a bloody pulp. There were two problems with that happening. First being I was injured and would likely fall before reaching him and second, I didn't come to fight him, I came to understand him and my mother. I cleared my throat and said, "I just want to get to know my brother."

He glared at me and then spat on the ground. "Your brother's dead." He turned around and headed back into the garage.

I began to move towards him, but Kristen's hand grabbed my arm and she said in a whisper, "Don't do it, Kane. He's not worth it."

I looked back at her and said, "Oh, it'd be worth it. I'd destroy him before my mind would even let me feel the pain in my side. He can't talk about Kyle like that!" I snapped back at her.

Kristen looked over at Timothy. "You won't accomplish anything... and you'll never find out why your mom did it if you act on that impulse."

She was right. I relaxed myself and took a deep breath in. "Thanks..."

"Let's get out of here," she said, pulling my arm around in the driveway and leading me back to her car.

As we got in, I glared out the window down the driveway to where he was. "I don't get why people like that exist in the world."

She shrugged. "I don't know," Kristen replied. Turning the key over, we began to drive down the road.

"Wait, go back to the other house. I have an idea," I said.

"Okay." She turned the car around and drove back over to the first house we went to.

Jumping out of the car, I ran up to the door and knocked again.

"You again? What do you want?" The old man asked, angered.

"I couldn't tell Tim about the prescription."

"What do you mean?"

"He was out of control and rude."

The old man coughed and nodded. "That's how he gets when he starts drinking."

"Oh, he's not usually a drinker?" I asked,

hopeful.

The old man laughed in his raspy voice. "I reckon you are a little stupid, Boy. Tim gets rude everyday when starts drinking at about noon."

"Oh," I replied, with a saddened tone. "Do you need me to get the prescription? For Kyle?"

The old man narrowed his eyes. "Who are you? And why are you so interested in my boy, Tim?"

My eyes widened. "Tim's your son?"

"He's my nephew. But yes, he might as well be my son. Who are you?"

"I'm his brother..."

The old man furrowed his eyebrows, coughed and turned his back on me, slamming the door shut behind him. Knocking again on the screen as I heard the deadbolt lock, I shouted, "Please, Sir! I need to talk to you!"

"Kane," Kristen said from behind me.

I kept knocking as I became more angry and desperate. "Sir! Please!" I shouted. Turning around, I dropped down to sit on the steps and dipped my head into my palms.

Kristen came and sat beside me without saying a word.

Looking up at her after a moment, I was comforted by how beautiful Kristen was in the moment. She looked upset, just as much as I did. "I don't get why these people are treating me like this? Why would my mom leave all the money to Timothy?"

Kristen shrugged. "Again, I don't know..." She sighed. "Well, it sounds like he gets a late start. Maybe you can catch him before his drinking starts tomorrow?"

"I don't think being sober is going to change anything." I looked at my phone for the time. "It's barely after twelve thirty in the afternoon... I doubt he was already plastered." Standing up, I sighed and headed towards Kristen's car with her. Getting in, I looked back to the house and saw the old man peek his eyes out the blinds. "Maybe..."

"What?" she asked.

I grabbed a receipt from the glove box and wrote on the back of it the address and name of the hotel. I also added that I'd be leaving in the morning. Getting out of Kristen's car, I ran back up to the house and stuck it between the screen door and the door frame.

Getting back into the car, Kristen asked, "Just going to hope he shows up?"

"Nah..." I replied, shaking my head.

"Then, what?" she asked.

"I'm going back to the hotel to *pray* he shows up."

Kristen smiled and pulled away from the curb.

CHAPTER 17

After a long afternoon and making it partially into the evening, I began to give up hope that Timothy was ever going to show up. Then, we got a knock on the hotel door. Kristen and my eyes both widened as we leaped from our chairs at the table in my room. She went to the window and peeked out while I looked out through the peephole.

"Oh my gosh, Kane!" Kristen said. "He's here! It worked! Our prayers worked!"

I smiled and nodded over to her. Grabbing

the doorknob, I opened it.

"Hey," Timothy said in a soft tone.

"Hi," I replied. "You came."

Looking over at the window, he said, "Could we have that talk? Maybe without your girlfriend."

She hurried past me grinning and went back to her room. I smiled as I watched her unlock her door and go inside. She shot me a short wave before closing the door.

"Come on inside," I said, opening my door the rest of the way and stepping out of his way so he could enter.

"Thanks," he said, walking in past me. "Sorry about earlier... I was caught off guard when you showed up. I was scared you just wanted to show up and take my money. Later in the day, I got home and talked to my Uncle Mike and he said I should come see you. It might be the only chance I got. So I came."

"I see," I replied. That must be an adopted uncle or something, I thought to myself.

He went and sat down in one of the chairs at the small table in the room. He flipped over the glass ashtray and was about to light a cigarette. "Do you mind?" he asked.

I came over to the table and sat down. "I don't care." I reached over and opened up the window for ventilation. "So..."

He lit his smoke and tossed the lighter on the table. "What do you want to know?" he asked, pushing the smoke towards the window as he exhaled.

"Everything."

He laughed. "I don't have time for that. I have to get back to Kyle."

"First off, who's Kyle?"

He adjusted in his seat and leaned across the table as he set his smoke down in the ashtray. "He's my son."

"Okay. Did you name him after my Kyle?"

Timothy scoffed and shook his head. "Your Kyle? I think he was all of ours..."

"What do you mean?" I asked.

"We have the same dad. Mom just couldn't deal with me... so she gave me up."

"Why?"

"She was seventeen at the time."

"Wow," I replied, leaning back. "When did you meet my... I mean our mom? And how?"

He picked his smoke back up and took another puff. "She found me the first time about six years ago. Right after Kyle died."

"And why did you name your son after Kyle?"

His jaw clenched as he looked down at the table and shook his head. "My wife liked the name. Why do you care so much?" he asked, looking up at me with furrowed eyebrows.

"I'm trying to learn about you. I didn't know you even existed until you showed up at the will reading."

He pointed his smoke at me that was between his fingers. "I was at that funeral. I was in the back, laying low. Trying to be respectful to all that were there." He sniffed and wiped a runaway tear from his eye as he continued, "I loved mom in my own different kind of way. But I didn't condone what she did to you guys by not telling you about me."

"Wait. You said, 'the first time' was around the time that Kyle died. What happened with that?"

"I was bad into meth and I attacked her."

I recalled back around the time that Kyle had

died. I remember her specifically having a bloody-red eye that she blamed on a car door hitting her in the face. "Did you hit her in the eye or something?"

He nodded. "Yeah, with an ashtray... Kind of like this glass one." He pointed to the ashtray on the table. "That was a bad part of my life... I thought I'd never see her again after that."

"Then what happened?" I asked, scooting my chair closer to the table. "What changed?"

He shrugged and put out his smoke, saying, "She forgave me."

"She had a forgiving spirit."

"She reached out to me again after the cancer diagnosis, she wanted to see me."

"And she changed the will around that time... Did she tell you why?"

He shook his head and said, "I don't know why she changed it. I didn't even know she did that or had a life insurance policy to begin with," he replied.

"That doesn't make sense."

He shrugged and acted like he was confused about it.

"Wait. Your son... Kyle?"

"Yeah?"

"Does he have cancer? That old guy at your house said something about a prescription? Or is there something else wrong? I saw a ramp."

Timothy shook his head, "No. He doesn't have cancer... just has the flu. That ramp was there when we moved in. The previous owner had a wheelchair. I'm sorry I don't have any answers for you. I just literally saw her a couple times my entire life..."

"It's okay," I replied, confused. Why would she do this? What was it that I was missing?

Breaking into my thoughts, Timothy stood up and asked, "Hey. You want to meet Kyle?"

I nodded. "I'd like that."

Walking into Kyle's bedroom back at Timothy's house, I opened the door to find him playing. "This is your Uncle Kane," Timothy said.

I smiled.

Kyle looked up at me for a moment and then continued playing. Bending a knee down to see what he was doing, I saw he was playing with a red fire truck. I couldn't help but smile again. "You like fire trucks?"

"Yeah," the little boy said followed by a flemmy cough.

Looking up at Timothy, I asked, "How old is he?"

"Five."

"You're five, Kyle?" I asked.

He nodded as he let another cough out. Then he held up the fire truck to my face.

"He loves fire trucks. Ever since our mom gave him that he has been in love with the idea of being a fireman some day."

I smiled, thinking about my mother. I sensed she knew I'd be here some day. Looking back at Timothy, I asked, "You know I'm a firefighter?"

He shook his head. "No. I had no idea. Mom didn't tell me about you and Emily very much... just said she loved you and you two were doing well." He looked down at Kyle. "You hear that? Your uncle Kane is a firefighter!"

Kyle looked up at me and said, "You a fireman?"

I nodded and smiled. "I am."

"Cool!" he exclaimed.

Standing up, I looked over at Timothy and said, "Thanks for bringing me to meet him. It's getting late, though."

"No problem. I'll walk you to the door." As we were walking down the hallway, I noticed holes along the hall in the wood paneling on both sides. And as we made it to the front door, I stopped and turned to Timothy.

"Emily's going to contest the will most likely," I said.

He nodded. "I figured you both would contest it."

"You don't seem mad about that," I said, confused.

He shrugged. "I don't care a whole bunch about money. As you can see."

"Why?" I asked.

He sighed and stepped outside, shutting the door behind him. "Money has never done anything outside of be a means to an end for me. And honestly... do you want to know the truth?"

"Well, duh." I replied laughing.

"I did know about the money..."

I dropped my smile and shook my head. "You lied to me?"

"Not exactly... The truth is, mom had a very specific reason for the money to come my direction. She wrote this letter about what she wanted done with the money. It feels more like a laundry list than anything else and if you guys take the money, I won't have to deal with some hard ones on the list." He reached into his back pocket and handed it to me. "It's all in there."

"Why wouldn't she entrust Emily and I with this letter?" I asked.

"Just read it," Timothy insisted.

The door behind him opened and it was Kyle. "Daddy... can you make me some dinner?"

He nodded as he went inside. He paused before shutting the door and said, "That's a copy. Take it and read it. If it ends up uncontested... I'm going to go ahead and do what the letter states. I couldn't go against mom like that... if it's contested, I'll just take my own portion and do what I want. Ya know... since I won't have enough to do the stuff in the letter. Up to you, brother."

I nodded and headed down the steps and back out to Kristen's car. Getting in the car, she asked, "What's that you have?"

"I don't know, I haven't read it." Looking down at the letter, I began to read it out loud.

Dearest Timothy,

I am leaving my entire life insurance policy, in the sum of $500,000 to you. Every dime that you receive, I'd like for you to spend on what this letter states. If you choose not to spend it as I wish, that is your choice. I pray that you do the right thing.

> *1.   Please move into a nice house. Part of the life insurance policy can easily afford you a decent house in the current area you live. I looked into the prices.*
>
> *2.   With another piece of the money, please enroll Kyle in a private Christian School*

for grades of kindergarten through sixth grade.

3. Use a portion of the money to return to school and make something of your life. You can do anything you want.

4. Buy a decent car

5. Pay Emily back for my funeral expenses (I'm sure she went all out and would appreciate it).

6. This one doesn't cost money, but my hope is you do it. Spend at least 12 months going to church, reading your Bible and listening to Christian music. While this is the only

> *item on the list that doesn't cost money, it's by far the most important and valuable.*

Love,

Your Mother

My eyes watered and I wiped the tears away as I looked over at Kristen. "This is what I needed to find."

"Is this your mother's handwriting?"

I nodded.

"You think he'll do it?" she asked, glancing back up towards the brick house with a concerned look on her face.

"I hope he does..." I replied. Thinking about Emily, I worried about what she would say. It didn't say anything about us getting any cut of the money outside her funeral expenses.

CHAPTER 18

Pulling up to the curb at Emily's house back in Spokane, Kristen put the car into park. Glancing out the window towards my sister's house I smiled and then looked back over at Kristen. "Thanks for going with me... Or... I guess taking me." I laughed.

She smiled and looked through the windshield. "I enjoyed going."

Leaning over the armrest, I gently turned her chin with my finger to face me. She looked deep into my eyes and I into hers. Slowly leaning in closer, my lips touched hers momentarily. It was perfect. Leaning back in my seat, I broke out in a smile.

"That was..." she took a deep breath. "Nice."

"It was." I leaned in again, this time quicker and I slid my fingers through her hair as I pulled her in for a passionate kiss. Stopping myself, I released and grinned. "We should stop."

"Yes, we should," she replied, blushing as she took another deep breath. "I'm going to head over to Moses Lake and pick up Blake."

"Good. Is he ready to come home?" I asked.

She nodded. "I talked to him a little bit yesterday when you were speaking with Timothy."

"That'll be good for him to get back home," I replied, trying to continue the small talk to keep my mind off the kiss. Looking over at Emily's house, I saw her looking out from the window in her living room.

"She's kind of creepy," Kristen said, laughing, and leaning down to see a glimpse of Emily through the windshield.

"I know," I replied. "She loves being all up in my business." Reaching over to the door, I opened it. "Thanks again. And... when can I see you again?" I asked, not wanting to leave.

"Friday night? I think the youth is doing basketball at the church. We can go do something during that time," Kristen said as I got out of the car.

Looking Kristen in the eyes, I nodded. "Alright," I said, smiling.

"Kane," Emily said from the steps of her house behind me.

"I better go," I laughed. Leaning into the car I grabbed my duffle bag from the back seat.

"See you around," Kristen said, putting the car into drive.

Shutting the car door, I turned around and began walking up to Emily. She looked confused as she watched Kristen drive away. "What happened to your car?"

"It's totaled."

Her eyes widened. "You aren't upset?"

"I'm extremely upset, but not much I can do about it."

"What happened?" Emily asked.

"Few days ago I got into a wreck and ended up in the hospital."

"What? The hospital? Why didn't I know

about this?"

I shrugged. "You don't need to know everything that happens."

"You were hospitalized!" she retorted.

"I was out of there the same day I went."

"Really?" she asked, looking me up and down.

"Yeah..." I paused. "I saw Timothy..."

Her eyebrows shot up. "Come inside."

Following her in, I tossed the duffle bag on the couch and took a seat next to it. Kicking my feet up on the coffee table, I relaxed back into the couch and my eyes began to grow heavy with exhaustion.

"So... tell me about what happened with Timothy," Emily said.

I put my feet down and sat up. Leaning down to pet Roofus, I pulled the letter from my back pocket and handed it to her. She began reading the letter and covered her mouth as she gasped. Setting it down, she wiped her eyes with a Kleenex from the coffee table.

"Hey, Uncle Kane," Christopher said, walking in from the hallway.

"Sup? I heard you went to another LAN party with the youth?" I asked, watching him walk into the kitchen.

"Yep, " he replied as he opened up the fridge. "It was a blast."

"That's good."

"Do you know when Blake is coming home? We missed him..." Christopher asked, pulling out a pitcher of orange juice. "I only ask because I saw you getting out of Kristen's car out my bedroom window."

I stood up and joined him in the kitchen. "Kristen just headed off to go get him from Moses Lake."

"You two an item now?" Emily asked from the living room couch.

Looking at her trying not to show too much of my boyish excitement, I said, "I think so."

"Good for you. She's hot," Christopher said.

"Christopher Allen!" Emily snapped at him.

"Sorry... she's really attractive?" Christopher said, smiling.

I laughed.

"Can you come back in here so we can talk about this?" Emily asked me, looking at the letter.

I turned and looked at her, "Sure."

Coming back into the living room, I took a seat on the couch. She waited for Christopher to finish getting his snack and retreat back to his room. As the door shut, she turned to me, "So. Do you buy this letter?"

"What? Of course... it sounds like mom."

She sighed. "Yeah... and it's in her handwriting... Seems real."

"But he can't do it if we contest the will..." I replied.

"Why's he need all this money?" she asked, holding out the letter. "Is it that bad for him?"

"Ems... he has holes in his wood paneling."

"Wood paneling?" she asked, looking remorseful. "Holes? That bad?"

I nodded. "It's bad."

"What about your car? And my student loans? We have needs too..."

I put my hand on Emily's and said, "This money can change his life." I shook my head, "We aren't going anywhere if we get that money, we both have careers, and we already had all the opportunities we needed growing up, Ems. He didn't get that."

She sighed as she seemed to be thinking it over, looking at the letter again. "Okay. You're right. I can't believe I'm saying this, but let's let him have it. I won't contest it."

I smiled and hugged her. "You're doing the right thing, Ems," I said.

"For the record... I think he's going to blow it all and not do anything in this letter. But it's what mom wanted."

"I'm going to pray he does it," I replied.

"Hey. Do you want mom's Oldsmobile so you have wheels?" she asked.

"What about Christopher? She left that to you so he could have it."

Emily laughed. "I'm not worried about it. He's not driving for a while and you need a car."

I nodded. "Want to give me a ride up there to get it?"

"Of course, how else are you going to get it?" She replied, laughing.

I shrugged grinning. "Thanks, Sis."

"I never thought I'd see the day you'd drive something like that around... maybe you *have* really changed," Emily replied.

Getting into my mother's old car took me back to a simpler time. Kyle, Emily and I would all load up in the back seat and go visit Aunt Colleen over in Lincoln City. It was a twelve hour drive one way and we didn't have much money for hotel stops so we'd have to do a straight shot there. We'd get in the car before dawn right after breakfast and drive all day to make it there in time for dinner. It worked out so we only would be eating one meal on the road, lunch.

Turning the key over, I smiled as it fired up without any complaints. My cell phone rang as I watched Emily pull out of mom's driveway. It was Cole.

"You called me earlier, but I missed the call," Cole said.

"Yeah, I was seeing if that baseball game with

the station was going on yesterday or today."

"It happened yesterday."

"Dang... I missed it."

"Yeah. Did you find your brother?" Cole asked.

"I'll stop by the station and tell you all about it."

As I climbed the stairs of station 9, the smell of Micah's stew filled my nostrils and I got a good feeling deep inside, like I was home again. Reaching the dining hall, I smiled as I saw all the guys sitting around the table sharing a meal.

As I walked in, everyone stopped eating and stood up. Each one of them offered their condolences individually. My eyes welled with tears as each one of my brothers shook my hand and gave me a hug. As they sat back down, Cole turned in his chair and said, "Grab a bowl, McCormick. The stew is still hot."

Going into the kitchen, I smiled as I poured

myself a bowl of the stew. These guys had my back no matter what. As I sat down at the table next to Brian, he asked, "You coming back to work?"

"Of course," I replied. "I just saw you the other day and told you that. I'm thinking Monday, next week."

"Four more days," Rick said.

"Good math, Alderman," I replied with a laugh. "But it's actually five days. Today is Wednesday."

"Chief said you could take a couple weeks off, though, right? It's only been a week," Cole said before taking a bite of his stew.

"That is true," I replied. "But I'm feeling up for returning earlier... We already did the funeral. Just not much more to do. I don't have a whole lot of family around."

Everyone nodded in acknowledgment with their mouths full.

Taking a bite of my roll and then a spoonful of stew, I smiled. I sure did miss the home cooked meals here at the station, I thought to myself. Looking up, I made eye contact with Micah. "My car is totaled."

"No way, man!" Micah responded, shaking

his head. "What happened?"

"Got hit on the way out of my apartment complex. I was at a dead stop and some bozo in a truck nailed me," I replied.

"Did you get hurt?" Ted asked.

"Yep. Check this out," I replied. Standing up, I lifted up my shirt and showed them my bandage. Peeling it back, everyone cringed, but Ted, he leaned in for a better look.

"Not while we're eating, man!" Rick snapped.

I laughed and sat back down. "Sorry about that."

"You thought you could play baseball with a wound like that?" Cole asked.

"It doesn't hurt too bad and I just try to ignore it. I would have been fine, I think."

"But twisting your whole body when you swing a bat would be killer on that wound."

"True... I didn't think about that. That'd probably hurt."

As I was putting my disposable bowl in the garbage after dinner, Cole came into the kitchen. "You seem great, Kane. You been relying more on

God?"

"Yes, Sir. That talk up on the mountain changed my life, man."

He shook his head. "You were already on the right path."

I put my hand on Cole's shoulder. "No... That was incredible what you did for me up there. I went back to my mom's and repented and began digging into God's word. The most incredible things have happened since I started letting the Holy Spirit lead me."

Cole replied, "I noticed a change in you even from the other day I saw you at your apartment. You were upset that day, but I sensed the change. So tell me what happened with your brother."

"He needs the money bad," I said. Pulling out the letter, I handed it to him, and said, "My mother left him that letter and I got Ems to not contest the will. So I'm hoping and trusting God will help Timothy do the right thing. And if he doesn't... I'll be okay with that too."

Cole read the letter and handed it back to me. "That's amazing, McCormick." He nodded. "I hope he does it. That'd be awesome!"

I nodded and pushed him lightly in the

shoulder. "Hey. Guess who got saved?"

"Emily?" Cole asked.

I shook my head. "She's on the way to the cross I have a feeling. But no, Christopher."

"Christopher? That's great!" Cole replied, beaming.

"I know. Isn't that awesome?" I asked, putting the letter back in my pocket.

"God is good!" Cole replied, looking up.

"He sure is... Thanks again. For everything."

"Anytime you need anything, let me know," Cole replied.

"Same goes for you, Cole."

"Thanks," he said as he began putting the stew in a plastic storage container.

My phone rang, pulling me away from Cole. Walking out into the hallway, I saw it was Christopher.

"Hey, Bud," I said, answering.

"Hi, Kane."

"What's going on?" I asked as I walked into

the weight room.

"Just wanted to call and see how you were doing. Mom told me about your car getting destroyed... that super sucks."

I smiled. I knew how much Christopher loved my car. "It does suck, but I'm thankful to God nobody got seriously hurt."

"Speaking of God. I was wondering... how do you get people to agree with you?"

I laughed as I sat down on an exercise ball in the weight room. "What do you mean?"

"This kid keeps trying to tell me God doesn't exist... and he wants to argue all the time."

"I see... You'll run into that from time to time on your walk with Christ."

"So... what verses should I tell him?"

I slipped off the side of the ball and dropped my phone. Picking it back up, I moaned in pain.

"What's wrong?" Christopher asked.

"I fell off this medicine ball in the workout room at work."

He laughed. "Why were you on it?"

"Just doinking around while I talk to you. I'm fine. But back to that kid arguing with you... I'd just try to show him kindness and love."

"He's a jerk, though," Christopher replied.

"Yeah. But you want to be different than the world. He wants to get a rise out of you. Just keep showing kindness to him. If he doesn't believe in the Bible, verses won't do much for him."

"Christopher!" Emily shouted from the background.

"I gotta go. Mom's calling for me out in the living room," Christopher said, exasperated.

Sensing his agitated tone, I said, "Be nice to your mom. She works hard to provide for you. And remember, you can call me anytime."

Hearing the smile in his voice, he replied, "Thanks, Uncle Kane."

"You're welcome," I replied before hanging up the phone. I couldn't help myself from smiling as I wondered what God had in stored for that kid.

CHAPTER 19

Arriving at Kristen's house that Friday evening, I parked along the curb in front to pick her up for our dinner date. Looking in the mirror at the sweat beading on my forehead, I told myself it's okay and it's the middle of August, of course it's going to be hot. And if a little warmth in a button up shirt is all I have to endure to look nice for Kristen, I'm okay with that. I got out of the car and headed up the path to the front door. I could see her through the living room window. Looking in a mirror that hung on the wall, she looked stunning. The way the low lighting of a lamp in the room played off her skin, she looked divine.

Knocking on the door, I stood back and held the bouquet of daisies behind my back. I had noticed on our trip that she had an air freshener in her car that was of the same flower. It was a hunch, but I suspected she probably liked them regardless.

The door unlocked and she opened it. My heart warmed at seeing her smile and I handed the bouquet to her. She turned red and took a deep breath in to smell them. Smiling, she looked up at the flowers and said, "I love daisies!"

"Good," I replied with a grin.

"Come on in, I just need to grab my necklace really quick and then we can go."

"Alright," I replied, stepping inside and shutting the door behind me.

She set the flowers down on the island in the kitchen and headed down the hallway. Glancing through the sliding glass door off her kitchen, I could see through her yard and into the park. I put my hands in my pocket and thought back to that day Christopher and I had gone to play baseball. Just an uncle and his nephew tossing the ball around and enjoying the sunshine. If we never went there, I might have never seen Kristen again. Wow.

Coming back from the hallway, she asked, "What are you smiling about?"

I nodded towards the sliding glass door. "If the power would not have gone out that day we saw each other at the park... we might not have ever seen each other again."

She nodded. "It's weird to think about... isn't it?" She laughed. "I remember being so mad the power went out... but now, I'm glad it did," she said. Handing me her necklace, she asked, "Could you?"

I smiled as I took the necklace in my hands and brought it to her neck. As I put it on her, I said, "I can't believe that was only a few weeks ago."

Looking up at me as she turned, she looked me in the eyes and placed one hand on my chest as she said, "I feel like I've known you forever, Kane."

I laughed a little out of embarrassment more than anything else. "C'mon..." I said.

"Seriously. The way you were able to handle the thing with your brother... And all the miles we went to go see him. When I talk to you I feel connected to you more than I've ever felt with another person. It's crazy..."

I tipped my chin in acknowledgment and smiled at her as I put my hands around her waist. I brought my hands up the sides of her and to her hair. Running my fingers through her flowing blonde hair, I leaned in and kissed her. Everything felt so right. So perfect. It was like we were meant for each other. Stopping ourselves before letting it get too out of control, we released from our embrace.

"We should get going," I said with a short nod.

She smiled and went over to the flowers on the counter. "Let me get these daisies in a vase and then we can leave."

"Okay," I replied, walking into the living room.

"Your text earlier said Emily was okay with Timothy having the money, but you didn't say why," she said as she removed the flowers from the packaging.

"She knew it was my mother's letter and succumbed to my mother's desire to give him the money I guess. She wanted it, but she knew it was the right thing to do. I like to think it was God reaching through." I smiled.

Kristen turned on the faucet and began trimming the ends of the daisies. "That's great! I think you're right. She was pretty determined to contest it. I think Timothy will do the right thing."

"Me too," I replied, smiling over at her as I saw her put the flowers in a vase. "I think it's the first time she's ever put faith in a person... I hope it works out."

Kristen set the vase on the counter and arranged the daisies so they looked pretty. Looking at them for a moment and then up at me, she smiled. "Reminds me of a sermon my father preached a couple weeks back. He focused the message on Jesus, but more specifically the faith everyone had put in Him at the time he walked the earth."

"I haven't ever thought about Jesus in that light. We have the cross and resurrection now, but they –the disciples and followers of Christ— were trusting in Him before the resurrection."

She nodded as she picked up her purse and came around the island to join me in the living room. "It was a pretty neat message. I sure love getting up there to Colville and getting to hear some of his preaching once in a while."

I smiled. Putting my arm out for her to grab, she latched on as I opened the door and led her out to my mother's old car.

Pulling out a chair from the table for Kristen, I caught her staring out the large bay windows that overlooked the falls and the Spokane River. "Beautiful, isn't it?" I asked.

She sat down and set her purse next to her chair as I rounded the table to sit across from her. "It is. I love the view of the falls," she replied, smiling at me.

I could stare into those eyes all night, I thought to myself before the waiter arrived, breaking my stare.

"Good evening," the waiter said, arriving at the table with menus. After handing us the menus, he flipped our elegant water glasses over and filled them each with ice water. "Tonight's special is a pan-seared wild Alaskan salmon. Could I get you started with a few drinks?"

"I'll take a strawberry lemonade," Kristen said as she looked at the menu.

"I'll just take a few slices of cucumber to go with my water please," I said.

"Very well," he said, bowing as he left our

table.

"Jeez... this place is fancy, Kane," Kristen said in a whisper across the table to me.

"You're a classy gal, I thought you'd like it," I replied, grinning.

She smiled as she looked at the menu.

"When's your vacation over?" I asked as I spotted the Char-Grilled Burger on the menu. Closing my menu, I folded my hands over the top.

She sighed. "Tomorrow..."

"Yeah, I'm going back on Monday. I'm ready to hop back into the action."

She looked up at me and asked, "They didn't give you more time off?"

"The Chief said I could take more time, but I don't need it. I've grieved and made my peace. It's time to start moving forward."

"That's good."

"Krissy?" Tyson said out of nowhere.

We both looked over to see Tyson coming over with a surprised look on his face. "Oh, jeez," Kristen said as she put her hand to her forehead. "I'm sorry," she mouthed to me as he approached.

I smiled at her shaking my head to signal it was fine as we turned to greet Tyson.

"Hi, Tyson," Kristen said.

"Hey." He looked over at me and shook my hand. "I know you from somewhere... right?"

"Yeah. The youth barbeque at your church. I had the Shelby..."

"That's right!" He exclaimed, pointing to me. "How are you doing?"

"Good," I replied shortly.

He turned back to Kristen and said, "I have someone I want you to meet. Let me take you over there."

Kristen glanced over at me. I smiled, and tipped my chin as she got up to join him. They went across the restaurant back to his table. He had a woman with him at the table. Sweet, I thought to myself. He's moving on from 'Krissy.' Turning, I looked out at the falls that were raging just outside the window below. Watching as I saw people walk across the top, I thought about my mother. She might have been gone now, but just like those falls, her soul would continue on.

"Sorry about that," Kristen said, sitting back down to our table.

Looking at her, I shook my head, "No problem. He has someone new he's infatuated with?"

She nodded as she glanced back towards their table. "Cynthia. It's one of the other youth group moms from another church... so that's good."

"I agree," I replied, relieved that it wasn't just his sister or something.

The waiter came back over to our table and took our orders. As he was leaving our table, Kristen asked, "How do you do it?"

"What?" I asked.

"Stay so calm... Like, about your mom and Tyson..."

I shrugged. "What should I do? I just give it to God. I know He has a plan and everything will work out one way or another."

Her eyebrows shot up. "You're right, but I'd be beside myself if my dad had died."

"Yeah..." Leaning in, I asked, "Where is your mom? I never hear you speak about her."

"She left my dad a long time ago when I was five. She didn't like him being a preacher. She couldn't handle it."

"Wow... I'm sorry."

"It's okay, really. I talk to her from time to time, but there isn't a bond there. She lives up in Vermont."

"You ever see her?" I asked.

She shook her head. "Not very often. I've been up there a few times over the years, but she's pretty obsessed with her new husband and his boat."

"That's rough... I guess that's why we just have to rely on God and not other people."

"Easier said than done sometimes," Kristen replied. "But yes, that's what we should be doing."

I picked up my water and tossed a slice of cucumber in. "Yeah..." Taking a sip of the water, I set it back down. "Life's too short to waste it on being upset. I don't want to live that way. And I know my mother wouldn't want me to live that way either."

"You didn't freak out at all?"

Recalling my drunken stupor with Roofus, I laughed.

"What?" she asked, leaning in.

"I did freak out when I first found out about my mom..." I adjusted in my seat. "I got drunk and took my mom's dog for a walk up on a mountain."

She busted out laughing. Covering her mouth with a napkin to clean up the lemonade, she apologized. "I'm so sorry! That just sounded funny to me for some reason."

I grinned and looked out the window. "It was pretty funny."

"How'd that end up?" she asked.

Looking back at her, I said, "I fell into a ravine and fell asleep. Cole found me."

"Oh jeez," she replied, shaking her head.

I nodded. "Cole showed me the truth about God that next morning when I woke up. He told me it was my faith in God that was going to get me through the struggle... not the worldly vices."

"Yep," she replied with a short nod. "I had a crisis of faith when Blake's father bailed on us."

I leaned in and took a sip of my water. "Go on."

She shook her head. "That's okay..."

"Come on, Kristen. Why not?"

"It's embarrassing."

I shook my head. "My sister told you everything about my past and I just told you about the drunken dog walk."

She laughed, and said, "Okay." Taking a sip of her lemonade, she set it down and scooted closer to the table and leaned in. "After everything fell apart, I went out with my friend Elly that same night. We went to this weird rave party thing downtown and shots were flowing. I ended up drunk and face first in my dad's front yard."

"Oh, wow! Really?" I replied.

"Yeah... And the worst part was the entire church was there the next day to surprise him in the morning with a gift basket! I was mortified!"

I began to laugh trying hard not to show it.

She laughed too. "It's not funny!"

"How'd you move on past that and establish a relationship with your dad?" I asked.

"Well, once he learned of my ended relationship, he had me and Blake move in up there. I had to live by all the same rules I had when I was a kid."

"Bet that was fun," I said sarcastically.

"No! I loathed it. But I didn't have any choice

in the matter. Blake's dad peaced out of state and vanished, and I was stuck with a $2,000 monthly house payment and a kid to pay for."

"You didn't have a job?" I asked.

She shook her head as she took another sip of her drink. "No. He didn't want me working at all."

"Do you like working now?"

She shrugged. "I didn't mind not working, honestly. But I kind of ended up in a really bad spot by not having a job in that situation. But it worked out. Living at my dad's got me back into church and I found a job at a diner up there in Colville."

"Which one?" I asked.

"Lucy's," she replied.

"Oh, we used to go there all the time. My mom loved their eggs benedict breakfast."

Kristen nodded. "That's the best one. What was your mom's name again?"

"Marilynn."

"Oh. I don't think I waited on her... or at least don't remember doing so."

"Really? She was in there all the time. She went by Mary sometimes?" I replied.

"No..." Kristen's eyes widened.

"What?"

"She went by Mary?"

"Yeah, wait... do you remember her?"

Kristen reached down into her purse and pulled out a coin. Handing it to me with a trembling hand, she said, "She gave me that coin after we had a few different conversations about God. She said it was her good luck charm and a reminder that God and her son she lost at war, were always with her. I didn't want to take it, but she insisted. She helped me through my struggles I was having with my faith. I always keep it with me. Do you recognize it? Was it Kyle's?"

Looking at the coin, my eyes widened. It was *the* coin. A military navy coin that she bought in San Diego on her trip to see Kyle graduate. One side read: **Navy, United States of America** and on the other side: **This we'll defend. Joshua 1: 9 Be strong and of good courage, do not be afraid, do not be discouraged, for the Lord your God is with you wherever you go.** Looking up at her, I asked with watery eyes, "Yes... When did she give you this?"

"About three years ago or so...?"

It was after Kyle died. My mom gave this coin away? And had given it to Kristen? "Wow..." I replied, relaxing back in my seat as I stared at it.

Kristen wiped away a tear from her eye as she shook her head. "She was the most gentle spirit I have ever met in my life, Kane." She sniffled and looked me in the eyes as she continued. "It was a difficult time because I felt so alone, like Blake's dad took all of me and just left the ashes from the fire he caused in our family's life. The one thing she told me that stuck out the most was the fact that God is an artist and he can use our ashes to shape us into beautiful works of art. She said I was a work of art and I needed to let God mold me in His image. I have let Him rule my life ever since then. She really moved me." Wiping away another tear, she said, "I'm sorry."

"No..." I said, reaching across the table to touch her hands. "I'm happy you met her. And she helped you." I was mystified how much my mother had helped Kristen. I could not help but marvel at God's timing. My mom had no idea how much Kristen would mean to me one day, but God did. My eyes watered thinking about how much God loved me.

Thinking about the fact that Kristen was at the funeral, I wondered how she didn't see a picture anywhere. "How did you not realize it was her at the funeral?"

Kristen shrugged. "I guess I was just busy in the kitchen. I was trying to give you your space. I swear I had no idea..."

I picked up the coin on the table and looked at it again, shaking my head.

"You can have it," she said.

"No," I replied, handing it back to her across the table. "Keep it. She gave it to you."

She smiled. Taking the coin back, she put it into her purse. As I waited for the food to come, I looked back out the window at the falls and thought about my mother. It warmed my heart to know she had met Kristen before and that they shared a bond together. My mother had helped her in a crucial part of her life and I never knew about it. My mind began to wonder how many other people were out there like Kristen that she helped. Strangers, who just happened to cross her path and she showed them Jesus. She was inspiring me, even beyond the grave.

CHAPTER 20

A call came into the station only thirty minutes into my shift on Monday morning. Leaping into action, I darted from the dining hall with the guys to the fire pole. Getting on my turnouts in the bay, I leaped onto the ladder truck.

"Bet your adrenaline is soaring like crazy. It's been a long time," Micah said as he pulled out of the station and onto the street.

"Like an eagle!" I shouted with glee.

"So your flesh wound is okay?" Brian asked from beside me.

I nodded. "It's a little sore, but nothing to worry about."

"Good. Because you're doing the ventilation cuts today," Brian replied.

I laughed, tilting my head as I looked over at him. "I'm gone for a couple weeks and Rookie gets a little cocky?"

Cole turned in his seat to look back at me. Smiling, he said, "Gomer has been stuck doing ventilation cuts since you've been gone."

"It's not too bad making the cuts, but it's annoying when Sherman and Alderman look up as they pass under and ask me if I enjoy watching real fireman work," Brian said.

I laughed.

"It was funny the first time. I'll give them that much," Brian said, laughing. "But after a few times... it gets old."

"I'll do the cuts, and gladly do them as I watch them pass under me." I was just happy to be back with my brotherhood. Looking out the window, I saw Old Man Smiles out my window walking down the sidewalk. I waved to him as we turned onto Riverside Ave.

"You know that guy?" Cole asked, looking back from his window towards me.

"Kind of," I replied, grinning recalling his rhyming way of talking.

Getting to the fire scene, I leaped out of the truck and came around to the side to retrieve the chainsaw and a ladder. As I unlatched the compartment door, Rick came over to me.

"Do you remember how to do this?" he asked, laughing as he patted my shoulder.

I laughed, looking over at him. "Yeah, yeah... Laugh it up, Alderman." I smiled. "Maybe after this when we get back to the station I can give you some math lessons?" Ted laughed on his way past us with the hose.

Putting the ladder against the one-story house, I climbed up with the chainsaw in hand. As I walked across the roof, I could see Rick and Ted running the hose to the front of the house. Brian was back near Cole and the trucks talking to the house owners. Thankfully nobody was trapped inside, so search and rescue weren't going to be needed.

Firing up the chainsaw, I made the cuts

needed on the roof and the chunk fell through and into the house. Backing up as I turned off the chainsaw, black smoke billowed out from the opening.

"Careful," Brian said from behind me on the ladder.

I looked back at him and said, "I don't remember that much smoke being normal."

He laughed as he came up on the roof. "Little rusty, aren't ya?"

"Nah," I replied, shaking my head.

Suddenly we fell through the roof and into the house. Coughing, I looked around and called out to Brian. "Gomer!" I shouted.

He coughed and made a moan.

"You okay?" I shouted as I began to stand up.

"I think so."

"Where are you?" I asked, glancing around the living room we had fallen into.

"Over here," he shouted.

Climbing through the roof debris, following the sound of his voice, I found him on top a burnt up couch. Once I realized he wasn't badly hurt, I began to laugh.

Cole came in and saw us. "Why you lying down on the job, Gomer?" Cole asked sarcastically.

Rick peeked in beside Cole. "Rookie," he said, shaking his head.

Brian laughed and began to get up. Limping a little as we began to walk out. I asked, "What hurts?"

"My arm."

"Stop limping," I replied, laughing.

He smiled and stood up as we walked out. As we came outside of the house, we both were still coughing some from the smoke exposure.

"Your arm okay?" Cole asked, touching Brian's shoulder.

He nodded. "I think it just got bruised."

"Okay." Cole looked towards the ambulance. "Go get it checked out by one of the paramedics anyways."

Brian began walking over to the ambulance that was on scene. Coming over to me, Cole asked, "You good?"

I nodded as I glanced back at the remains of

the house that were still intact. "Glad there wasn't a fire billowing below us when we fell through."

"Thanks to Sherman and me," Rick said, smacking my shoulder firmly. "Good to have you back, but try to not destroy the houses we are trying to save next time." He grinned.

I smiled over at Rick and nodded. "I'll try."

After getting cleaned up back at the station and showered, I went down to the bay to start swabbing the floors. Mop duty was mine for the week following my return to work.

Halfway through mopping the floors, I heard a woman's voice come from beyond the bay doors around the corner. It was faint and I wasn't able to hear what she was saying. Setting my mop back in my bucket, I walked to the bay doors and peeked outside.

It was Kristen and my heart pumped a little harder at the sight of her. She was further down the sidewalk and trying to open the exterior entrance door that was locked. "Hey," I said, waving to her.

She had Blake with her.

"Hi," she replied, looking my way before she began to walk down the sidewalk. Coming up to me she kissed my cheek and said, "Is it okay I stopped by? I wanted to see you and I have something for Cole."

I nodded. "That's fine."

She looked at my bandaged eyebrow from where I got hurt from my fall. "You okay?" she asked, touching the side of my face. Her touch was so comforting.

"Of course," I replied. Looking over at Blake, I said, "Did you have a good summer?"

"It was pretty cool in Moses Lake. Ate a lot of fast food and swam a ton."

"I bet that was cool."

He nodded. "We played baseball a couple times too."

I grinned. "Nice."

"How's it going, Kristen?" Cole asked as he came out from the bay.

"Good, how are you doing, Cole?" she asked.

"Good, good."

"Megan and the boys?" she added.

"They're good too," he replied.

"Here's the pamphlet you wanted," she said, handing Cole a folded piece of paper.

"What is that?" I asked, as I watched her give it to him.

"For the men's retreat. Remember? At the barbeque you got a pamphlet on it," Cole said.

I nodded. "Yeah, I remember now."

Looking over at Kristen, Cole said, "Thanks for this. I think Rick and Brian are just about to give in and come along with us."

"Really?" I asked. "I knew Alderman had some church background, but Gomer?"

Cole nodded to me. "God is good, man. Gomer started letting me talk to him more about God last week. It's a work in progress... but it's a step in the right direction."

"Wow. I'm impressed," I replied.

"Well, I gotta get going... but I'm glad I got to see you," Kristen said, touching my arm.

I leaned in and kissed her cheek. "It was nice to see you too. I'll see you around."

Kristen smiled and turned with Blake to leave. As they vanished around the corner up the street, Cole stepped up next to me. "You two together now?"

I nodded as I kept my eyes locked ahead. "Sure am... I think this one is going to stick."

Cole patted my shoulder and said, "So do I."

CHAPTER 21

Fall descended on the city of Spokane and for a few of us at Fire station 9, that meant it was time for the men's retreat in Suncrest. The town was small and located just outside of Spokane in the Nine Mile Falls area. Piling into Cole's new Tahoe; Cole, Micah, Brian, Rick and myself all journeyed up to the retreat.

"Wow... Those leaves are pretty," I said, looking out the window at the tops of the trees along the river road leading up to Suncrest.

"Pretty?" Rick laughed.

I glanced over at him and rolled my eyes. "What's a better term? Manly?"

"The word 'awesome' is good for a guy to say," Brian chimed in with all seriousness. Looking past me at the trees, he added, "They are awesome looking trees."

I laughed. "Okay."

Micah and Cole were in the front seat laughing softly amongst themselves. Micah looked back from the passenger seat up front and said, "Keep it together boys, we're just about there."

Cole looked in his rearview mirror at us and grinned.

"What?" I asked, making eye contact with Cole.

"You guys back there are less behaved then my children."

Rick leaned forward and said, "You put me with a couple of kids in the back seat, I'm going to get a little cranky!"

Cole laughed. "Sit back, Justin. I don't want to tell you again!" He busted out laughing at the reference to him being his four year old son, and everyone joined in.

Rick sat back and went red in embarrassment.

Coming to the entrance of the retreat, we pulled up to the main office. Cole and Micah headed into the office while the rest of us got out of the car.

Looking across the entire retreat, I marveled at the facilities they had. A large logged cabin sat down by the lake and nestled itself up against a forest.

Coming up behind us all, Micah pointed over to the cabin. "That's the Fireside Lodge and where we will be staying with a few other churches from Spokane."

"Wow," I replied, smiling over at Micah. "That's huge."

"It's nice inside too..." Micah replied.

We all grabbed our suitcases from the back of the car and began making our way across the grounds over to the cabin. As we came near the lake, Rick pointed at the boats and rafts. "Too bad we didn't get to come here when it was warmer."

"You can always sign up for a Summer one next year, Alderman," Micah said.

He nodded as he grumbled and stepped over a log.

Reaching the cabin, we walked inside to the foyer. Micah pointed to a hallway. "This will be our wing of the lodge. Find yourself a room and get your stuff in there. Breakfast will be served in the Dining Hall, which is located further down the lake. Should be available right now."

"I thought I saw a forest just beyond this lodge though?" I said.

"There's a path through the trees. You can't miss it if you head that direction. You go past the Chapel lodge and the Dining Hall is just beyond that."

I nodded. "Thanks, Micah."

After getting my suitcase unpacked and my clothing put away in my room, I headed for the dining hall for some breakfast. On the way through the woods, I noticed the sun shining through the tops of the trees just like it did up on the mountain in Colville. I smiled, thinking of my mom and all that she had done for me. I had come so far from the man I once was.

Coming up the steps into the dining hall, I was met by a kind looking older man. He held open the door and said, "Welcome."

"Thank you," I replied, shaking his hand.

When I stepped into the hall, I could smell eggs, bacon and hash browns in the air. I felt myself jump a little inside with excitement for the meal ahead of me. I was starving since I had woken up so early to prepare to come up here. Getting through the line and a plate of food, I went and found a seat near the bay windows that overlooked the lake. The peaceful and calm morning water was beautiful.

Grabbing the pepper that was next to the napkin holder on the table, I sprinkled it over my eggs and hash browns before bowing my head to pray. Thanking God for the food and the time I was going to have over the weekend, I was filled with joy. Opening my eyes from my prayer, I was surprised to see Tyson standing in front of me.

"Hi, Tyson," I said.

"Hey, Kane..." he replied, sitting down directly across from me.

He looked conflicted and after a few minutes

of me eating and him not talking, I set my fork down and wiped my mouth with a napkin before asking, "What's up?"

"I wanted to apologize," he said, softly.

"For what?" I asked.

"The way I acted with Kristen. I know it wasn't good for you two. But I'm happy now and when I saw you sitting over here, I wanted to make it right between us."

I shook my head. "We're cool. I didn't hold it against you."

He laughed. "Come on... I see you at church all the time. You always have that look. Like you're mad at me."

Looking out the window at the lake for a moment, I thought about it. He was right. I was holding onto that. Turning my attention back to him, I extended out my hand for him to shake and said, "Okay... Well, thank you for coming over and apologizing. I accept your apology."

He grabbed my hand and said, "No problem. Are you excited for the guest speaker? He should be taking the stage up front within the next few minutes."

"Someone is speaking during breakfast?" I

replied.

He nodded. "It was a last minute thing, I heard."

Suddenly I saw Timothy over near the stage. "What's he doing here?" I asked.

Getting up from my seat, I began walking over until he took to the stage. Stopping, I looked at him, but he didn't see me.

Getting up to the microphone, he tapped it with his finger. "This thing on?" he said. It boomed his voice across the room. "Yep," he laughed.

I sat down at a nearby table in the crowd and listened.

"Hi. My name is Timothy Raton and I want to spend a couple minutes sharing my story with you while you eat." He looked across the room and said, "I want to tell you today about how one person changed my life."

I thought about my mother and smiled. Another success story about my mom's unyielding contribution to God's Kingdom, I thought.

"Kane McCormick," he began to say. "Is my brother. Doesn't seem like a big deal, right?" He glanced around the room. "Well, for me, it's a huge deal. You see, I was given up as a newborn baby. I didn't know who my parents were or why they gave me up. I just knew I wasn't wanted. This fact alone set me on a path. Not because I wanted it to, but because I allowed it to dictate the next thirty eight years of my life."

He sniffed and wiped a tear from his eye. "My mother visited me when I was in a bad spot for the first time ever. I was meth'd out and I hurt her." He got choked up on his words and paused while he re-composed himself. "I thought that was it for her in my life. That I had ruined it... but she came back into my life, when she got sick with cancer." His lips perched as his bottom lip quivered. "Sorry. Anyways... Turns out she left me all this money in her will. She cut her other kids out, entirely. I didn't understand it and honestly, I didn't care." He wiped another runaway tear. "I was just going to spend the money how I pleased at first, and ignore the letter that detailed how she wanted it spent. She gave me that letter one of the last time I saw her. Then, Kane showed up. He was my brother and he wanted to get to know me. He fought for me like my mother could have, but never did." He paused and said, "I don't know if I'll ever see him again, but I do know that God is real. And He loves each and every one of us. I know this truth because I experienced God first hand. I treated Kane, my brother, like garbage and he still came for me, fought to know me. That's God-sized love that isn't humanly possible in my eyes."

I was shocked. I stood up and he noticed me. His eyes widened as we made eye contact. "Kane?" he asked, tilting his head, his eyes began watering as the crowd clapped.

"Yeah," I replied, smiling up at him on stage. Walking through the crowd, I joined him on stage and gave him a hug.

"I tried calling you to see how everything was going..." I said in his ear.

As we released from the hug, he shook his head and said, "I got off my uncle's plan and got a new number." He smiled at me. "I'm doing everything in the letter."

"I'm so happy for you, Brother."

Releasing from our hug, I looked out to the crowd and spotted Emily standing near the back. She was clapping and crying as I made eye contact with her. What was she doing here? I was so overwhelmed that the question didn't linger long. I wanted her up here with us. Motioning for her to come on stage, she began weaving through the crowd towards us.

Coming up to the stage, she looked at me as she smiled. "You were right all along about having to experience God. And when I found out that Timothy really had changed, I knew everything you said was true, Kane. And I believed right there in that moment," Emily said, crying as she leaned in and hugged me.

"I'm so glad, Ems!" I shouted over the sound of the crowd as I hugged her and wept.

When we released from our hug, she hurried over to Timothy and hugged him too. Looking across the dining hall, I saw Cole standing off to the side. He gave me a nod and I knew right then that he had orchestrated the entire thing. As the crowd grew more excited of God's presence over the retreat, my heart warmed and I thanked God for all that He had done for me.

The curtain behind the stage rose up behind us and Kristen stepped out to the microphone. I was completely floored. She began singing 'Holy Spirit' by Francesca Battistelli. Stepping off the stage with Timothy and Emily by my sides, I smiled. My mother's hope was for others to experience the glory of God's goodness and she accomplished it. She was affecting lives even though she was gone. Her testimony and love for our Lord and Savior continues to shine through the lives she touched.

My brother, nephew and sister all came to know the Lord within weeks of losing our mother. From out of the ashes, God created beauty and exchanged our pain for hope. Our mother might have passed onto Glory. And we will die someday also, but the truth and the power that is in the Word of God will last forever.

BOOK PREVIEW

Preview of "The Perfect Cast"

Prologue

Each of us has moments of impact in life. Sometimes it's in the form of *love*, and sometimes in the form of *sadness*. It is in these times that our world changes forever. They shape us, they define us, and they transform us from the people we once were into the people we now are.

The summer before my senior year of high school is one that will live with me forever. My parents' relationship was on the rocks, my brother was more annoying than ever, and I was forced to leave the world I loved and cared about in Seattle. A summer of change, a summer of growth, and a summer I'll never forget.

Chapter 1 ~ Jess

Jess leaned her head against the passenger side window as she stared out into the endless fields of wheat and corn. She felt like an alien in a foreign land, as it looked nothing like the comfort of her home back in Seattle.

She was convinced her friends were lucky to not have a mother who insisted on whisking them away to spend the *entirety* of their summer out in the middle of nowhere in Eastern Washington. She would have been fine with a weekend visit, but the entire summer at Grandpa's? That was a bit uncalled for, and downright wrong. Her mother said the trip was so Jess and her brother Henry could spend time with her grandpa Roy, but Jess had no interest in doing any such thing.

On the car ride to Grandpa's farm to be dropped off and abandoned, Jess became increasingly annoyed with her mother. Continually, her mother would glance over at Jess, looking for conversation. Ignoring her mom's attempts to make eye contact with her, Jess kept her eyes locked and staring out the window. Every minute, and every second of the car ride, Jess spent wishing the summer away.

After her mother took the exit off the

freeway that led out to the farm, a loud pop came from the driver side tire and brought the car to a grinding halt. Her mom was flustered, and quickly got out of the car to investigate the damage. Henry, Jess's obnoxious and know-it-all ten-year-old brother, leaned between the seats and glanced out the windshield at their mom.

"Stop being so annoying," Jess said, pushing his face back between the seats. He sat back and then began to reach for the door. Jess looked back at him and asked, "What are you doing?"

"I'm going to help Mom."

"Ha. You can't help her; you don't know how to change a tire."

"Well, I am going to *try*." Henry climbed out of the car and shut it forcefully. Jess didn't want this summer to exist and it hadn't even yet begun. If only she could fast forward, and her senior year of high school could start, she'd be happy. But that wasn't the case; there was no remote control for her life. Instead, the next two and half months were going to consist of being stuck out on a smelly farm with Henry and her grandpa. She couldn't stand more than a few minutes with her brother, and being stuck in a house with no cable and *him*? That was a surefire sign that one of them wasn't making it home alive. Watching her mother stare blankly at the car, unsure of what to do, Jess laughed a little to herself. *If you wouldn't have left Dad, you would have avoided this predicament.* Her dad knew how to fix everything. Whether it was a flat tire, a problematic science project or her fishing pole, her dad was always there for her no matter what. That was up until her mother walked out on him, and screwed everybody's life up. He left out of the country on a three month hiatus. Jess figured he had a broken heart and just needed the time away to process her mom leaving him in the dust.

Henry stood outside the car next to his mother, looking intently at the tire. Accidentally catching eye contact with her mother, Jess rolled her eyes. Henry had been trying to take over as the *man of the house* ever since the split. It was cute at first, even to Jess, but his rule of male superiority became rather old quickly when Henry began telling Jess not to speak to her mother harshly and to pick up her dirty laundry. Taking the opportunity to cut into her mom, Jess rolled down her window. "Why don't you call Grandpa? Oh, that's right... he's probably outside and doesn't have a cell phone... but even if he did, he wouldn't have reception."

"Don't start with me, Jess." Her mother scowled at her. Jess watched as her mother turned away from the car and spotted a rickety, broken down general store just up the road.

Her mom began to walk along the side of the road with Henry. Jess didn't care that she wasn't invited on the family trek along the road. It was far too hot to walk anywhere, plus she preferred the coolness of the air conditioning. She wanted to enjoy the small luxury of air conditioning before getting to her grandpa's, where she knew there was sure to be nothing outside of box fans.

Jess pulled her pair of ear buds out from the front pouch of her backpack and plugged them into her phone. Tapping into her music as she put the ear buds in, she set the playlist to shuffle. Staring back out her window, she noticed a cow feeding on a pile of hay through the pine trees, just over the other side of a barbed wire fence. *I really am in the middle of nowhere.*

Chapter 2 ~ Roy

The blistering hot June sun shone brightly through the upper side of the barn and through the loft's open doorway, illuminating the dust and alfalfa particles that were floating around in the air. Sitting on a hay bale in the upper loft of the barn, Roy watched as his nineteen-year-old farmhand Levi retrieved each bale of hay from the conveyor that sat at the loft's doorway. Each bale of alfalfa weighed roughly ninety pounds; it was a bit heavier than the rest of the grass hay bales that were stored in the barn that year. Roy enjoyed watching his farmhand work. He felt that if he watched him enough, he might be able to rekindle some of the strength that he used to have in his youth.

While Roy was merely watching, that didn't protect him from the loft's warmth, and sweat quickly began to bead on his forehead. Reaching for his handkerchief from his back pocket, he brought it to his forehead and dabbed the sweat. Roy appreciated the help of Levi for the past year. Whether it was feeding and watering the cattle, fixing fences out in the fields, or shooting the coyotes that would come down from the hill and attack the cows, Levi was always there and always helping. He was the son of Floyd Nortaggen, the man who ran the dairy farm just a few miles up the road. If it wasn't for Levi, Roy suspected he would have been forced to give up his farm and move into a retirement home. Roy knew retirement homes were places where people went to die, and he just wasn't ready to die. And he didn't want to die in a building full of people that he didn't know; he wanted to die out on his farm, where he always felt he belonged.

"Before too long, I'll need you to get up on the roof and get those shingles replaced. I'm afraid one good storm coming through this summer could ruin the hay."

Levi glanced up at the roof as he sat on the final bale of hay he had stacked. Wiping away the sweat from his brow with his sleeve, he looked over to Roy. "I'm sure I could do that. How old are the shingles?"

A deep smile set into Roy's face as he thought about when he and his father had built the barn back when he was just a boy. "It's been forty years now." His father had always taken a fancy to his older brother, but when his brother had gone away on a mission trip for the summer, his dad had relied on Roy for help with constructing the barn. Delighted, he'd spent the summer toiling in the heat with his dad. He helped lay the foundation, paint the barn and even helped put on the roof. Through sharing the heat of summer and sips of lemonade that his mother would bring out to them, Roy and his father grew close, and remained that way until his father's death later in life.

"Forty years is a while... my dad re-shingled his barn after twenty."

"Shingles usually last between twenty and thirty years." Roy paused to let out a short laugh. "I've been pushing it for ten. Really should have done it last summer when I first started seeing the leaks, but I hadn't the strength and was still too stubborn to accept your help around here."

"I imagine it's quite difficult to admit needing help. I don't envy growing old –no offense."

"None taken," Roy replied, glancing over his shoulder at the sound of a car coming up the driveway over the bridge. "I believe my grandchildren have arrived."

"I'll be on my way then; I don't want to keep you, and it seems to me we are done here."

"Thank you for the help today. I'll write your check, but first get the hay conveyor equipment put away. Just come inside the farmhouse when you're done."

Roy climbed down the ladder and Levi followed behind him. As Roy exited the barn doors, he could see his daughter faintly behind the reflection of the sun off the windshield of her silver Prius. Love overcame him as he made eye contact with her. His daughter was the apple of his eye, and he felt she was the only thing he had done right in all the years of his life on earth. He'd never admit it to anyone out loud, but Tiff was his favorite child. She was the first-born and held a special place in his heart. The other kids gravitated more to their mother anyway; Tiffany and he were always close.

Parking in front of the garage that matched the paint of the barn, red with white trim, His daughter Tiffany stepped out of the driver side door and smiled at him. Hurrying her steps through the gravel, she ran up to her dad and hugged him as she let out what seemed to be a sigh of relief.

Watching over her shoulder as Jess got out of the car, Roy saw her slam the door. He suspected the drive hadn't gone that well for the three of them, but did the courtesy of asking without assuming. "How was the drive?"

"You don't want to ask..." she replied, glancing back at Jess as her daughter lingered near the corner of the garage.

Roy smiled. "I have a fresh batch of lemonade inside," he said, trying to lighten the tension he could sense. Seeing Henry was still in the backseat fiddling with something, Roy went over to one of the back doors and opened the door.

"Hi Grandpa," Henry said, looking up at him.

Leaning his head into the car, Roy smiled. "I'm looking for Henry, have you seen him? Because there's no way you are, Henry! He's just a little guy." Roy used his hand to show how tall Henry *should be* and continued, "About this tall, if my memory serves me correctly."

Henry laughed. "Stop Grandpa! It's me, I'm Henry!"

"I know... I'm just playing with you, kiddo! I haven't seen you in years! You've grown like a weed! Give your ol' Grandpa a hug!" Henry dropped his tablet on the seat and climbed over a suitcase of Jess's to embrace his grandpa in a warm hug.

"Can we go fishing Grandpa? Can we go today?"

Roy laughed as he stood upright. "Maybe tomorrow. The day is going to be over soon and I'd like to visit with your mother some."

Henry dipped his chin to his chest as he sighed. "Okay." Reaching into the back trunk area of the car, Henry grabbed his backpack and then scooted off his seat and out from the car. Just then, Jess let out a screech, which directed everyone's attention over to her at the garage.

"A mouse, are you kidding me?" With a look of disgust, she stomped off around Levi's truck, and down the sidewalk that led up to the farmhouse.

"Aren't you forgetting something?" Tiffany asked, which caused Jess to stop in her tracks. She turned around and put her hand over her brow to shield the sun.

"What, mom?"

"Your suitcases... maybe?" Tiffany replied with a sharp tone.

Roy placed a hand on Tiffany's shoulder. "That's okay. Henry and I can get them."

"No. Jess needs to get them." Roy could tell that his daughter was attempting to draw a line in the sand. A line that Roy and his late wife Lucille had drawn many times with her and the kids.

"Really, Mom?" Jess asked, placing a hand on her hip. "Those suitcases are heavy; the men should carry them. Grandpa is right."

Henry tugged on his mother's shirt corner. "I think you should let this one go, Mother." He smiled and nodded to Roy. "Grandpa and I have it."

Tiffany shook her head and turned away

from Jess as she went to the back of the car. "She's so difficult, Dad. I hate it," Tiffany said, slapping the trunk. "She doesn't understand how life really works."

"Winnie," Roy replied. "Pick your battles." The nickname *Winnie* came from when she was three years old. She would wake up in the middle of the night, push a chair up to the pantry and sneak the honey back into her bedroom. On several occasions, they would awaken the next day to find her snuggling an empty bottle of honey underneath her covers.

"I know. It's just hard sometimes, because everything is a battle with her lately."

"She'll come around. You just have to give her some time to process everything."

Chapter 3 ~ Jess

Kicking her shoes off on the front patio, Jess noticed a hummingbird feeder hanging from the roof's corner. A small bird was zipping around the feeder frantically. She smiled as she thought of her friend Troy, back in Seattle. He was a boxer and often referred to himself as the hummingbird.

Entering into the farmhouse, Jess glanced around and saw that nothing had changed since she had been there five years ago. The same two beige couches with the squiggly designs on the fabric sat in the living room, one couch on each side. The same pictures of all the family hung behind the television. And even the picture of her grandmother, Lucille, which sat on the mantle above the fireplace, right between the wooden praying hands and the shelf clock. Everything was the same.

Walking up to the picture of her grandma, she looked at it longingly. *Why can't mom be like you were, Grandma?*

Hearing Henry and the rest just outside on the patio, Jess quickly made her way across the living room, through the dining room and through the door leading up the stairwell to her room she knew she'd be staying in. The wood paneling on both sides of the hallway leading upstairs made her laugh. *He has the money from Grandma's life insurance, yet he updates nothing.* It was so old and outdated, but then again, everything was in the house.

Lying down on the daybed that was pushed up against the lone window in the room, she turned on her side and peered out the window. Pushing the curtain back, she could see down the hillside and a faint view through the trees of the creek. She couldn't help but recall playing in it with Henry and all her cousins, years ago.

They would sneak pots and pans from the kitchen when grandma wasn't looking and journey down the hillside with them to the creek. They were *farming for gold* as they often referred to it. Looking back over her childhood, she couldn't help but have a longing for the simpler times. Grandma was alive, mom and dad were together and all the cousins lived in the same city. She hated being forced by her mother's hand to be at the farm this summer, but she loved the childhood memories that came with being there.

Hearing the door open at the base of the stairwell, Jess slid off the bed. She suspected her mother was going to be calling for her.

"Come down and visit with your grandpa," her mother hollered up the stairs loudly. Jess came out of the room and looked down the stairs at her mom.

"You don't have to yell..."

"Just come downstairs and visit, please." Her mother left the door open and walked away. *It was hot up here anyway.* Jess missed a step on her way down the stairs and tumbled to the bottom.

"Ooouuuchhh!" Jess said, grabbing onto the arm that she had braced herself with on the fall. Glancing up, she was greeted by laughter from a rude, but very attractive, brown-haired boy with the bluest eyes she'd ever seen.

Extending a hand to help her up, he said, "I'm sorry, but that was just too funny."

Jess pushed his hand out of her way. "I'm glad my pain can be of entertainment to you." Pushing herself up off the steps, she stood up and looked at him. "Who are you?" she asked curiously.

"I'm Levi. I live up the road and help Roy out with the farm. I know you're Roy's granddaughter, but I didn't catch your name...?"

"I'm Jess... I had no idea other people lived out here our age. How do you stand to live without cell phones and cable?"

"What's a cell phone?" Levi laughed. "I'm

only kidding. You just get used to it." Jess nodded as she proceeded past him.

Entering into the kitchen, she grabbed for a clean glass from the dish rack and poured herself a glass of ice water. Taking a drink, she looked over to the table to see Henry, her mother and grandpa all staring at her.

"What?" she asked.

"Don't be *rude* with your tone Missy," her mom said. "But are you okay? We heard you fall down the stairs."

Jess's back and arm were hurting a little from falling, but she didn't want to let her mother get the satisfaction of nurturing her. "I'm fine, Mom."

"Ok. Well, your Grandfather and Henry are going to fish over on Long Lake tomorrow morning; did you want to join them?"

Jess immediately thought of her dad. In fact, every time she heard the word *fish* since the split, she'd think of him. Even the stupid commercials on television that were just ads for fishing supply businesses triggered it. She and her father would go on fishing trips at least twice a month during the summer, and sometimes even more. Last year, they had entered a fishing competition on Lake Roosevelt and had won first place. They got a trophy and a cash prize. It put them that much closer to their dream of getting a *real* fishing boat, instead of the duct-taped-up aluminum canoe they had gotten as a hand-me-down from Roy. It barely floated.

She was already upset that she had to be at the farm all summer; she wasn't going to give her grandpa or mother the satisfaction of her going fishing with him. They knew she enjoyed fishing, and that'd be a win for their column. "No." She turned to her grandpa and narrowed her look at him. "I won't be fishing at all this summer. I'll wait for dad to get back to do my fishing." Taking another drink of her water, she finished it and slammed the cup down in her frustration, and then exited the kitchen, angered she'd been even asked to go fishing.

Jess knew her grandpa most likely had some hand in her mother's decision to walk out on her father, and it infuriated Jess. He always had a dislike for Jess's dad. Jess thought it had to do with the day when the three of them had all gone fishing together and her grandpa never got as much as a bite on his hook. Yet her dad, in all his awesomeness, reeled in three that same day.

On her way back to the stairs, she saw into the living room that her luggage had been brought in. Unfortunately, the rude boy was sitting on a couch near her luggage. *Oh great, another encounter with prince charming.* As she grabbed her bags, he lowered his newspaper and looked at her beaming with a smile.

"Why do you insist on smiling constantly?"

"I'm happy."

"I find that hard to believe. You live in the middle of nowhere and have, like, no life." Levi kept the smile on his face and brought the paper back up to read. Jess felt like she was a bit harsh with him. "I'm sorry. I didn't mean that. I'm just... really upset right now. Sorry."

"You don't even know me or my life. You're just a city brat and I'm just a country hick, so let's just keep our distance from each other."

"You think I'm a brat?"

"No, I don't think you are..."

"Good..."

"No, let me finish. I know you are a brat." He lowered his paper and glanced at her. "The way you carried on in there with your grandpa was horrible. I wouldn't be caught dead talking to anyone that way, let alone my own grandfather."

Jess shook her head with her tongue in cheek. "You know what? You're right. Let's keep our distance from each other."

Levi raised his paper back up to read, and she scowled at him. Her grandpa came into the living room and said, "Levi."

Setting his paper down, he stood up and walked into the kitchen with her grandpa. Her mom noticed the tension between them as she and Henry came in and sat on the opposite couch from Jess.

"What's that all about?"

"Nothing, Mom. Just a country boy living in a bubble."

"What happened?"

"Well... he laughed at me for falling, for starters."

Henry snickered.

"Stop that," her mom said to Henry.

"And then... he called me a brat."

Her mom couldn't help from smiling, but she covered her face in the attempts to hide it. "I'm sorry, dear... You should try to get along with him though; he's been helping your Grandpa a lot out here."

Jess sighed, shaking her head. *I should have*

just taken that offer of Tragan's. That would have made more sense than being here. "Sure, Mom," Jess replied, rolling her eyes. She and Tragan, her friend in Seattle, were going to room together after Jess had learned of the *summer at grandpa's* idea of her mom's. She figured she was eighteen and could do whatever she wanted; her mom couldn't stop her. But after looking into the cost of splitting rent on a two-bedroom apartment in Seattle, she decided against it. There was no way she would be able to finish her senior year, spend time with her friends and work all at the same time, so she elected to obey her mother. Thinking back on it now, she wondered if she had made the right choice.

Chapter 4 ~ Roy

Standing up from the kitchen table, Roy extended his hand and shook Levi's firmly. Every week, after writing him a check, they'd shake on it. There was no need for contracts or other paperwork miscellanies out in the back country. The people out there were trusted and relied on by their word and their handshake.

"Be sure to tell your father hello for me." Roy retrieved a pocket watch from his pants' pocket and placed it in Levi's hands. On the face, it had an etching of a train stopping to let people on, and the exterior was entirely made of gold. "I want you to have this. I picked it up from the flea market the other day, and when I saw it, I thought of you."

"What about it made you think of me?" Levi asked.

"Life is kinda like a train. Sometimes it stops; sometimes it goes, but along the way it's always on track going somewhere. When my train had stopped, you were there to hop on."

"I'm sorry, but that sounds quite ridiculous."

"Ridiculous or not, I want you to have it."

"I can't take this," Levi said, rubbing the

surface before trying to hand it back to Roy.

"Please take it. I'll be offended if you don't. Now, don't forget to tell your father hello for me."

"I will, sir. It's always a pleasure working with you." Heading for the side door that led out of the kitchen and into the porch, Levi turned to Roy. "You have your work cut out this summer with that girl."

Roy smiled. "I know." Patting him on the back, Roy said, "That's why I have God to help me." Levi nodded and proceeded out into the porch, shutting the door behind him.

Walking through the kitchen, Roy could hear his daughter and grandchildren conversing about him in the living room. Stopping, he leaned against the doorway and listened.

Jess laughed. "He belongs in a home. You know it, I know it... we all have known it since Grandma passed. It's just ridiculous that he's draining his retirement paying that stupid boy."

She sure doesn't like him.

"My dad isn't going to give up this farm, Jess, that's just the way it is. This farm is in his blood. Without it, who knows how long he'd hold on. Meadows down the block from our house in Seattle would be perfect for him... but I don't see it ever happening, and I don't know if I want it to, either."

Roy sighed heavily as he leaned against the door frame. *She's already looked into it?* As if the next minute aged him fifty years, Roy found himself exhausted. Going back into the kitchen, he took a seat at the table and glanced out the large kitchen windows that overlooked the front yard. He watched as Levi walked the sidewalk out to his truck.

"Grandpa?" Henry said, walking into the kitchen.

"Yes?"

"Do you miss your dad?" Henry asked, as he climbed up to a seat at the table. Reaching across the table, he snatched an apple from the bowl of fruit.

"Every day," Roy replied. Over the years it had gotten easier for Roy, not because he'd missed his fatherless, but because he'd learned to live with a hole in his life.

"I miss my dad... a lot," Taking a bite of his apple, Henry had a smile crawl on his face. "He should be back in town when we get back to Seattle though, so it's not *too* far from now."

Roy rubbed Henry's head as he ignored the

comment about Brandon entirely. "Are you ready to go fishing tomorrow?" Henry nodded as he took another bite of his apple. "How big of fish are you going to catch?"

Henry leaped up from his chair. Stretching one arm up as high as he could reach, he said, "This big!"

"Ha," Jess said, walking into the kitchen to the fridge. Opening the door to the fridge, she sighed heavily. Roy didn't keep much food that the kids would enjoy around the house; he had forgotten to fetch some for their visit. That was something that Lucille had always taken care of before the grandchildren would arrive.

"There's soda on the porch, I know how you kids don't enjoy lemonade much," Roy smiled, hoping it would be good enough.

Jess shut the fridge and opened the door leading into the porch. Leaning, she looked out and laughed. "Diet caffeine-free..."

Henry cringed as he heard his sister. "Gross, Grandpa."

"I'm sorry about that. We can get some food and stuff tomorrow. Henry and I will be sure to swing by the grocery store on the way back from fishing."

Jess was going to leave the kitchen, but stopped and looked at her grandpa. "There's really nothing to do out here."

"You could go for a walk on the hill, read, paint, and draw... Really, anything is possible out here if you put your mind to it."

"Cell phones and cable aren't possible, no matter how much you put your mind to it."

"That's true, but those things are just distractions. You have to embrace life out here without all that technology."

"Whatever," Jess said, rolling her eyes as she walked out to the porch.

"She stresses mom out," Henry said, looking intently at his grandpa. "We don't know what to do with her."

Laughing, Roy said, "Who's *we*?"

"Mom and I."

Roy furrowed his eyebrows. "You're ten years old. You don't need to worry about Jess. She's not your concern. That's your mom's territory." Henry nodded and got down from the table. Watching as Henry walked out of the kitchen, sadness overtook Roy. Henry was but a child, and he was attempting to fill a void that only a father could. Roy knew he had a long summer ahead of him, but more importantly, he knew God had a plan in the midst of the chaos and turmoil in those two children's lives.

Looking out the window at the chicken coop across the yard, Roy watched as Jess ventured over to it. It reminded him of Tiffany's fascination with the chicken coop when she was but a child. Back years ago when she was six, she'd go out every morning before breakfast and collect all the eggs. While she didn't have a fondness for the smells that resided in the chicken coop, she loved those chickens and hens dearly.

"How many hens do you have now?" Tiffany asked, coming into the kitchen and leaning her head over Roy's shoulder.

"We have twelve," Roy replied with a smile, watching Jess open the door and go in.

Tiffany took a seat at the table and Roy turned to her. "She's not as lost as you think she is, Winnie."

"You don't know how difficult it is..." Tiffany said, putting her hands to her forehead as she rested her elbows on the table. "She doesn't listen to anything I say, Dad, and she hates everyone and everything except her father and her friends."

Roy placed a hand on Tiffany's and brought

it away from her face. "She's just a teenager. You were there once."

"Nothing like this, Dad."

"I'm sure it's different, but it's still the same. Children go through phases in life and she's going through one right now. You add in the fact that--"

"I know," Tiffany interrupted.

Roy stood up from the table and kissed his daughter's forehead. "I love you, Winnie, and your children are going to be *okay*. Just trust that God is doing a work here."

Chapter 5 ~ Jess

Plugging her nose, Jess took one look around the chicken coop and almost vomited. Straw and feces littered the creaky wood-planked floors. Turning, she pushed the chicken coop door open and almost fell out trying to move quickly.

"Disgusting!" she shouted, tiptoeing out of the coop.

Looking across the yard, she could see her grandpa through the farmhouse kitchen windows. He was waving at her with a big silly grin on his face. She turned away and looked across the field just beyond the coop that held the herd of her grandfather's cattle. The field sat at the base of the hill. Glancing up the hill, she saw the big rocks sitting on top.

Jess and her cousin Reese would trek up the hill and sit on a particular rock, and look down across the vast and open valley. Years ago, their grandmother would pack them lunches and juice boxes to take on their journey up there. They never made it beyond the rocks before stopping to eat their lunches, and one of those rocks was where they would sit and eat every time they went. She and Reese stashed a lunch box with a few baseball cards, a couple of colorful rocks and one Pog slammer. Every summer they'd go and find the same rock and the lunch box. It was like finding treasure every time. *I wonder if it's still there.* She thought as she kept her eyes on the rocks.

Walking back over to the farmhouse, she went into the kitchen where her grandfather and mother were sitting.

"Can I borrow the car, Mom?"

Her mom looked at her phone's time and shook her head. "I need to get back on the road shortly. I am stopping in Spokane for a meal with an old friend."

"Cool mom, thanks again for abandoning us just like you did Dad..." and under her breath, she said, "I hate you." Jess began to leave the kitchen.

"Just a minute there, girl! That's not respectful of your mother. If you could be a bit nicer you might be able to take my work truck," Roy said.

Jess stopped, frozen in her tracks. It was a pivotal moment for her. She had to decide whether or not to accept the offer from her grandpa. On one hand, she knew that she *needed* a vehicle if she was going anywhere this summer, and that meant using her grandpa's truck. On the other hand, she didn't want to give him the satisfaction of helping her. She didn't want him thinking that his involvement in her mom and dad's split was okay or justified. She was torn.

"Really?" Jess asked. She couldn't come up with anything else to spit out.

"Yep."

"Ok..." Jess said, walking back into the kitchen. She decided to take the generous offer, but she wasn't going to be happy about it. Her eyes searched the counters for a set of keys. "Where are the keys?"

"How about an apology? To your mother?" Roy asked.

Jess's jaw clenched and she could feel her blood begin to boil as she tried to keep herself from screaming. Turning slowly to her mother, she smiled forcefully. "I'm sorry, Mother."

"And what about *me* being kind enough to use the truck?"

Jess's teeth ground a bit while she tried to keep the smile. Without opening her mouth, and through her teeth, she said, "Thank you... Where are the keys?"

"Right there," Roy said, pointing to the counter. There was a stack of mail, a screw driver and some magazines.

"I'm not seeing them."

"The screwdriver," Roy said with a laugh.

"Ohhh...." Jess forced another smile. "I see."

"You don't have to drive it if you don't want to. I'm just offering it. It ain't a beauty by no means."

"No, I understand... I want to drive it." Jess grabbed the screwdriver and darted out of the kitchen. Leaving the farmhouse, she walked quickly along the path out towards the garage when her grandpa opened the window from the kitchen.

"The truck is along side of the barn," Roy hollered.

"Thanks!" Jess shouted over her shoulder. *Ugh... I didn't have to thank him again.*

Coming to the barn, Jess found that the barn doors were opened and she ventured in for a moment. Looking up at the rafters, she was filled with a familiar feeling that had been lost in her childhood. Back then she had such little care for life and the problems of the real world, like high school. Glancing over to the upper loft of the barn, she saw hay bales and recalled building forts with her cousins. They'd stack bales that reached almost to the ceiling of the barn.

Snapping herself out of the memories, she

turned and left the barn, headed for the truck that was parked along the side. When she got to the truck's door, she couldn't get the door open. Kicking it, she began to scream in her frustration. It was so hot outside she could barely hold onto the handle to open the truck for more than a moment. "Come on!"

"Calm down," Henry said coming around the corner of the barn. "You sound like you are being killed, Jess."

"Shut it, twerp."

"Let me help." Henry came up beside Jess.

"Ha. I'd like to see you try," she replied, stepping out of the way of Henry.

Henry gave each of his hands a spit and rubbed them together. *Gross.* She watched as her brother used all his force in the attempts to dislodge the truck door's handle. It was useless. He stopped and began to look around, spotting a wooden rake stuck in the ground as if it had been there for a very long time.

"You are going to rake the truck?" Jess asked jokingly.

Henry remained silent as he dislodged the rake from the ground. It appeared to have sunk partially into the grass and dirt in the field. Brushing off the dirt, Henry came back to the truck and used the butt of the rake to jam it up into the door handle.

"Good try, but I don't—" Suddenly the door popped open. Henry stood proudly with his chest puffed out. "Thanks," Jess said.

"Pleasure helping you, madam."

"Trying to talk like a cowboy," Jess said with a laugh. "Even Grandpa doesn't talk like that."

Henry beamed. "It's fun to pretend."

"I'm sure it is; I use to do the same thing when I was younger. Thanks bro." Pretending and dolls use to be a huge part of Jess's life. All the way up until she hit ninth grade and Suzie Donaldson came over to visit after school one day. Jess could recall it like it had just happened. When Suzie came over, she had laughed at Jess's doll collection. That marked the turning point for Jess. She wasn't going to be a little kid who played with dolls anymore; she was going to be a *cool kid* like Suzie, and leave the dolls behind.

Jess climbed into the truck and shoved the screwdriver into the ignition. After turning the screwdriver over, the truck fired up loudly and she pumped the gas to get it going. "Yay..." she said sarcastically as she began pulling forward around the front of the barn.

"I wanna go, I wanna go!" Henry shouted as he ran alongside the truck.

"I'd love to let you... but I can't." Jess drove off, leaving Henry in the rearview mirror as she went down the driveway, over the bridge, and out onto Elk Chattaroy Road.

Did you enjoy this preview?
*Pick up a copy of **The Perfect Cast** today!*

OTHER BOOKS

Embers & Ashes Series

Amongst the Flames (Book 1)

Out of the Ashes (Book 2)

Up in Smoke (Book 3) Fall 2015

After the Fire (Book 4) Winter 2015

Love's Enduring Promise Series

The Perfect Cast (Book 1)

Finding Love (Book 2)

Claire's Hope (Book 3)

Dylan's Faith (Book 4)

Stand Alones

Love Again

Love Interrupted

Visit www.tkchapin.com for all the latest releases

Subscribe to the Newsletter for special Prices, free gifts and more!

www.tkchapin.com

AUTHOR'S NOTE

When you leave a review on a book you read, you're helping the author keep the lights on. Our books don't sell themselves, it's word of mouth and comments others have made. Simply visit Amazon and/or Goodreads and let others know how the book was for you. It'd help me greatly. Thank you!

ABOUT THE AUTHOR

T.K. CHAPIN writes Christian Romance books designed to inspire and tug on your heart strings. He believes that telling stories of faith, love and family help build the faith of Christians and help non-believers see how God can work in the life of believers. He gives all credit for his writing and storytelling ability to God. The majority of the novels take place in and around Spokane Washington, his hometown. Chapin makes his home in the Pacific Northwest and has the pleasure of raising his daughter with his beautiful wife Crystal. To find out more about T.K. Chapin or his books, visit his website at www.tkchapin.com.